Y0-BSL-474

SA RY
SACRAMENTO, CA 95814

4/2018

[美]玛丽·波·奥斯本

32

WINTER OF THE TCE WIZARD

寒冰巫师

主译:蓝葆春　蓝纯
翻译:李倩

WITHDRAWN FROM COLLECTION
OF SACRAMENTO PUBLIC LIBRARY

湖北长江出版集团
湖北少年儿童出版社

★ 名人推荐 ★

陈乃芳：美国麻省大学高级访问学者，曾任驻比利时使馆兼驻欧盟使团教育处参赞，北京外国语大学校长；第九、十届全国政协委员，政协外事委员会委员，中国高等教育学会高教管理研究会副理事长，中国教育国际交流协会常务理事，《国际论坛》杂志主编；由泰国王储授予名誉教育学博士、由英国兰卡斯特大学校长亚历山大公主授予名誉法学博士，并有多部论著。

亲爱的少年读者们：

你们好！最近我有机会阅读了一套英汉双语版的系列丛书，名字叫做《神奇树屋》(Magic Tree House)，作者是当今美国最著名的少儿读物作家之一——玛丽·波·奥斯本。几乎全美国的少年儿童都喜欢读她写的《神奇树屋》，把她当作自己的好朋友。我虽早已年过六旬，但是我和美国的小朋友们一样，一拿到这套书就爱不释手，不到两天就全部读完了。

你们也许要问：您为什么这么喜欢这套书呢？

我的回答是：首先，作者的创作思路紧紧扣住了小读者渴求知识、喜欢冒险、充满好奇和富于幻想的心理特点，成功地打造了神奇树屋这个平台。神奇树屋挂在森林里最高的一棵橡树的顶上，里面堆满了图书。它的神奇之处在于小读者翻开其中的任何一本书，指着书中的一幅插图许愿说"我希望到那里去"，梦想就能即刻实现。其次，作者充分发挥"魔法"的作用，轻松自如地引领读者穿越时空，周游世界。从见识白垩纪恐龙时的翼龙和冰河时代最凶猛的野兽剑齿虎，到体察今日的澳洲袋鼠；从了解美国早期荒凉西部的牛仔生活，到欣赏古代中国牛郎织女的传奇故事；从游览古埃及的金字塔到身陷2000多年前中国的秦始皇陵；从遭遇加勒比海的海盗到幸会东方的日本忍者；从历险维苏威火山的爆发到探秘亚马孙河的热带雨林……真是随心所欲，神游八方。再者，作者成功地塑造了杰克和安妮这一对小兄妹，通过他俩的所见、所闻、所思、所想和亲身历险，把历史故事、神话传说、科普知识、人文传统等栩栩如生地展现在读者面前，让你如同身临其境。最后，这套书不仅内容丰富有趣，而且文字浅显易懂，让人捧读之下，不忍释手。

为了把这套优秀的少儿读物介绍给全中国的中小学生，湖北少儿出版社特别邀请了我的老同学、老同事、老朋友蓝葆春爷爷和他的女儿——北京外国语大学的蓝纯教授负责全套丛书的汉语翻译。他们的译文既忠实于原文，又琅琅上口。所以我建议小读者们在阅读过程中先读译文，再读原文，这样一书两用，既增长了知识，又提高了英语，算是一举两得吧。

最后我想感谢两位译者请我作序，让我有了先睹为快的机会。也感谢湖北少儿出版社为全中国的中小学生们献上的这份大礼。

祝你们阅读愉快！

陈乃芳

目录

1 冬至

Winter Solstice

　　寒冷的北风嘎嘎地敲打着玻璃窗，衬得屋内暖和而温馨。杰克和安妮正在和妈妈一起做圣诞节饼干。杰克把一个星形的模具按进面团里。

寒冷的北风嘎嘎地敲打着玻璃窗,衬得屋内暖和而温馨。杰克和安妮正在和妈妈一起做圣诞节饼干。杰克把一个星形的模具按进面团里。

　　"嘿!外面下雪了!"安妮说。

　　杰克望向窗外,午后的天空,大片的雪花正缓缓飘落。

　　"你想出去吗?"安妮问。

　　"不太想,天马上就黑了。"杰克回答。

　　"是的,"妈妈说,"今天是入冬的第一天,也是一年中最短的一天。"

　　杰克的心咯噔一下。"那就是说今天是冬至了?"他问。

　　"不错。"妈妈回答。

　　安妮吸了口气,问:"冬至是什么意思?"

　　"是……"妈妈有点不知怎样解释。

　　杰克和安妮互相看了一眼,他们想起去年的夏天,魔法师梅林就是在夏至那一天请求他们帮助的。也许今天他同样需要他们的帮助。

　　杰克放下手中的模具,用毛巾擦了擦手,"妈妈,下雪了,出去玩一会儿肯定很棒。"

"出去也行，"妈妈说，"不过得穿暖和些。我要做完这些饼干，然后放到烤箱里烤。"

"谢谢妈妈。"杰克和安妮说着就跑到衣柜旁，迅速地穿上靴子，套上外套、围巾、手套和帽子。

"记得在天黑之前回来！"妈妈这样叮嘱。

"我们会的。"杰克回答。

"再见，妈妈！"安妮跟妈妈道别。

兄妹俩跑出屋子，来到寒冷的雪地上。他们穿过银装素裹的院落，向蛙溪湾进发，靴子踩在雪上发出咯吱咯吱的声响。

杰克刚来到树林边，就被眼前的美景怔住了。洁白的雪花盖在铁杉和松树的枝丫上，煞是好看。

"你看！"安妮指着两行从公路沿伸到树林的脚印说，"有人来过了。"

"看上去他们好像是从树林里出来，然后又折回的，"杰克分析道，"我们得快点！"如果神奇树屋今天回来了，他不希望被其他人先发现！

兄妹俩顺着两行脚印急速地穿过树林。

"等等！"安妮说着一把拉住杰克，躲在一棵大树后面，

"你看那边。"

透过飘舞的雪花，杰克看见两个身穿深色长外套的人正匆匆向一棵高大的橡树走去，而神奇树屋就停在那棵橡树上！

"哦！不！"杰克惊呼。

树屋回来了，但是被其他人先发现了！

"喂！"杰克喊道，"站住！"树屋是回来找他和安妮的，不是来找别人的！

杰克冲了过去，安妮紧跟在后面。杰克脚下一滑摔倒了，他赶忙爬起来接着跑。可是等兄妹俩跑到树下，那两个人已经爬上绳梯，消失在树屋里了。

"出来！"杰克大喊。

"这是我们的树屋！"安妮也大声抗议。

那两人把头从树屋的窗户里伸了出来。他们看上去也就十二三岁的样子。男孩子有着一头蓬松的红发和满脸雀斑，女孩子有着海蓝色的眼睛和黑色的长卷发。他们的脸蛋儿被冻得通红。他们看着杰克和安妮，哈哈人笑起来。

"好极了！"那个男孩子说，"我们是来找你们的，没想到倒让你们先发现了我们！"

"泰德！"安妮惊呼，"凯瑟琳！你们好！"

泰德是和莫根一起在卡默洛特图书馆工作的年轻的魔法师。凯瑟琳就是那位被施了魔法的海豹女孩儿，她曾在夏至那天帮助过杰克和安妮，把他们都变成了海豹。

杰克怔住了，他从来没有想过他们在卡默洛特的两位朋友有一天会来拜访蛙溪湾！"你们来这儿干什么？"杰克大声问道。

"上来吧，我们会告诉你们的！"泰德回答。

杰克和安妮迅速爬上绳梯。一进树屋，安妮就拥抱着泰德和凯瑟琳，她激动地说："我简直不敢相信，你们会来看我们！"

"很高兴见到你，安妮！"凯瑟琳说，"还有你，杰克！"她那双蓝色的大眼睛忽闪忽闪的。

"我也很高兴！"杰克害羞地说。他一直认为凯瑟琳是他见过的最漂亮的女孩儿。尽管她曾经是只海豹，但她真的可爱无比。

"我们是来找你们的！"泰德说，"我们从树屋出来，穿过树林，来到一条公路边。"

"但是那条路上充满了怪物！"
凯瑟琳接着说，"一个巨大的红色怪
物差点儿就把我们给撞了！它还发
出刺耳的喇叭声！"

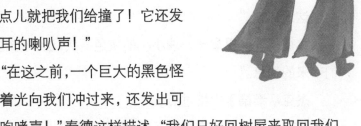

"在这之前，一个巨大的黑色怪
物闪着光向我们冲过来，还发出可
怕的咆哮声！"泰德这样描述，"我们只好回树屋来取回我们
的智慧。"

"它们不是怪物！"安妮笑着解释，"它们只是汽车！"

"汽车？"泰德一脸疑惑。

"没错儿，汽车有发动机，人可以开着车走。"杰克回答。

"发动机？"泰德还是不解。

"嗯，一两句话说不清楚的，"安妮说，"你们只要记住，在
我们的世界里，每次过马路的时候都要注意来往车辆。"

"嗯，我们会的。"泰德说。

"你们为什么会来这儿？"杰克又问。

"我们在梅林的房间里发现了一则给你们的留言，"泰德
说，"就决定亲自送来了。"

"我们爬进莫根图书馆旁边的树屋,"凯瑟琳说,"泰德指着留言上蛙溪湾这几个字说我们希望来这儿,然后我们就来到了这片树林。"

泰德从外套里拿出一块小小的灰色石头,说:"这就是我们带来的消息。"

杰克从泰德手中接过石头。

留言是用很小的字体手写的,杰克大声念出来:

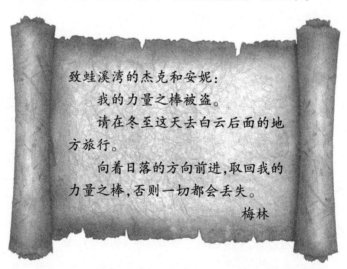

致蛙溪湾的杰克和安妮:
　　我的力量之棒被盗。
　　请在冬至这天去白云后面的地方旅行。
　　向着日落的方向前进,取回我的力量之棒,否则一切都会丢失。
　　　　　　　　　　　　梅林

"噢,天哪!"安妮说,"听起来很严重。"

"是啊！"杰克说，"但是梅林为什么不亲自把消息带给我们呢？"

"我们也不明白，"泰德说，"我们已经有好几天没有看到莫根和梅林了。"

"他们去哪儿了？"安妮问。

"这是个谜，"泰德说，"我是上周去海豚湾接凯瑟琳来卡默洛特的，她以后就在莫根的图书馆里帮忙。但是我们回来之后却找不到莫根和梅林。"

"我们只看到这则给你们的留言。"凯瑟琳说。

"嗯，我想如果梅林回来后，发现他的魔棒已经找回来了，一定会非常高兴，"泰德说，"他大部分的魔力都来自那根古老而神秘的魔棒。"

"哇！"安妮惊叹。

"在留言中，他让我们去白云后面的地方，"杰克说，"那会是什么地方？"

"那是在我生活的海湾北边很远的一个地方，"凯瑟琳说，"我从来没去过。"

"我也没有，"泰德说，"但我在莫根的书里读到过，那里

像白色冰冷的荒漠一样苍凉。我倒是挺想去看看的。"

"这么说你跟凯瑟琳会和我们一起去，对吗？"安妮问。

"对！"凯瑟琳回答。

"太棒了！"杰克和安妮异口同声。

"我们四个在一起，一定能够完成任何任务，对吧？"泰德说。

"太对了！"安妮回答。

希望如此吧，杰克心里暗想。

安妮指着梅林留言中"白云后面的地方"这几个字，问："大家都准备好了吗？"

"准备好了！"凯瑟琳回答。

"差不多吧！"杰克说。

"那就出发吧！"泰德催促道。

"我希望我们可以去这里！"安妮发愿了。

树屋开始旋转。

它越转越快。

然后一切都归于静止。

完全静止。

白云后面

Land-Behind-the-Clouds

　　杰克感到寒冷的北风刮在脸上生疼。他和其他人一起向窗外望去，"哦，天哪！"杰克不由得惊叹。

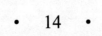

杰克感到寒冷的北风刮在脸上生疼。他和其他人一起向窗外望去,"哦,天哪!"杰克不由得惊叹。

　　树屋不是挂在树上——因为周围根本就没有树——而是落在一个高高的雪堆上。白雪覆盖着平原,雪堆此起彼伏。平原的边缘是丘陵和山区。

　　"书里说得对,"泰德说,他冻得牙齿直打颤。"这里真是荒凉!"

　　"不对,这里很美,"凯瑟琳说,"这里是北方的海豹人居住的地方。"

　　"很酷!"安妮赞道。

　　杰克把手插进口袋,他和泰德的想法一样。这里又荒凉又寒冷!"我在想梅林的力量之棒究竟在哪儿!"他颤抖地说。

　　"我们开始找吧!"凯瑟琳建议,"留言中说我们必须向着日落的方向前进。"

　　凯瑟琳爬出树屋。她把身上的斗篷紧了紧，在雪堆顶上坐下，用力一推，滑下了陡峭的斜坡。

　　"哦，哇！等等我！"安妮叫道。她跟在凯瑟琳后面爬出了窗户。只听"呼"的一声，安妮也滑到了雪堆下面。"你们快点来呀！很好玩的！"安妮高喊。

　　杰克和泰德看看对方。"我们也下去吗？"泰德问。杰克点点头。他把脖子上的围巾紧了紧，跟着泰德爬出了窗户。

　　杰克和泰德并排坐着。他们用力一推，一起滑下了冰冷的雪堆。杰克也兴奋得叫起来。真的很好玩。

　　到了雪堆下面，杰克和泰德挣扎着爬起来。杰克拍掉衣服上的雪，他发现可以在冰冷的空气中看见自己的呼吸。

　　"就是冷了点儿！"安妮说着抱住了自己。

　　只有凯瑟琳看上去不那么怕冷。她躺在雪地上，笑着仰望天空。也许是她的海豹的本能在帮助她抵御寒冷吧。杰克有点嫉妒她了。

　　泰德扫了一眼雪白的平原。"我想这里除了我们之外就再也没有生命了！"他说。

　　"一点儿都不对，"凯瑟琳说着指向天空，"我看见了雪鹅和呼啸而过的天鹅。"

"我好像也看见了。"安妮附和了一句。

凯瑟琳站了起来,目光从整个平原扫过。冰冷的太阳低低地挂在天空,在雪堆上留下蓝色的阴影。她指向远方,说:"在那儿,看见了吗?一只野兔正蹦蹦跳跳地往家赶呢。"

杰克看向凯瑟琳所指的地方,但他看不见任何东西在移动。

"我还看见了一头雪白的猫头鹰,"凯瑟琳接着说,"还有——哦,不!"

"怎么了？"安妮问。

"狼，"凯瑟琳颤抖地回答，"它们在一个雪堆后消失了。我们种族的人很怕狼。"

"你不用害怕，我会保护你的，"泰德拉起凯瑟琳的手，"来，我们快去追赶落日吧！"

泰德和凯瑟琳一起穿过白雪覆盖的平原，他们的羊毛斗篷在身后飞舞。安妮和杰克把手插在口袋里，迅速跟上他们，向着落日的方向前进。

当他们在冰冷的雪原上跋涉时，太阳慢慢落到地平线上，余晖给白雪染上了一层紫红色。

风吹打着杰克的脸。他低下头，继续往前走。寒冷的空气像针一样扎在他的皮肤上。每一次冰冷的呼吸都是痛苦的。他希望他们可以尽快找到梅林的力量之棒。他很难想象有人可以在这么寒冷孤寂的地方长久生存。

杰克的思绪被安妮的叫唤打断了。他抬起头。太阳已经完全落到地平线以下。在这寒冷的黄昏，原野上的积雪已经从刚才的紫红色褪成现在的深蓝。

"杰克！快来看！"安妮在叫唤。她正跟泰德和凯瑟琳一起站在一个巨大的雪堆的斜坡上。

杰克快步向他们走去。

"你看!"安妮说。

"哦,天哪!"杰克轻叹。

在雪堆的另一边有一座用大冰块砌成的宫殿闪着微光。在冉冉升起的月亮下,宫殿闪烁的尖顶划开了蓝色的天幕。

"我在想是谁住在里面……"杰克说道。

"我们进去看看吧!"泰德说。

他领着大家从斜坡上下来,向宫殿走去。长长的冰柱像长矛一样悬挂在入口的上方。

"看上去这里很久都没有人来过了!"凯瑟琳说。

"的确！"泰德说，"进去吗？"他说着敲断了几根冰柱，冰柱哐当掉在地上。

其他人都点了点头。

泰德踢开大块的冰柱，领着大家走进了冰宫。

寒冰巫师

The Ice Wizard

"欢迎你们，杰克和安妮！"一个声音从柱子后面传来。

杰克喘了口气。"是梅林的声音吗？"他小声问。

宫殿里面的温度甚至比外面还要低。月光透过高大的拱门洒了进来，地面光滑闪亮得像溜冰场一样。用晶莹的冰块做成的大柱子撑起圆形的屋顶。

"欢迎你们，杰克和安妮！"一个声音从柱子后面传来。

杰克喘了口气。"是梅林的声音吗？"他小声问。

"听起来不像梅林的声音！"泰德回答。

"那他怎么知道我们的名字呢？"安妮疑惑了。

"杰克和安妮，到这边来。我一直在等你们！"声音再次响起。

"说不定就是梅林呢！"安妮说，"他可能就是换了一种声音吧。咱们过去吧！"

"安妮，等等！"杰克喊着。但是安妮已经不见了。"我们得跟上她！"杰克对泰德和凯瑟琳说。

他们三个迅速地跟上安妮。在柱子后面，用冰雕成的台阶把他们带向一个高台。一个大胡子男人坐在高台上的宝座上。

他绝对不是梅林。他穿着一件用脏皮毛缝制的破旧长袍。他有一张饱经风霜的、苍老的脸，浓密的胡子，还带着一

个黑色眼罩。他身体前倾,用一只眼睛盯着安妮。

"你是谁?"他责问。"我在等来自蛙溪湾的杰克和安妮。"

安妮向宝座迈进一步,说:"我就是安妮,他是杰克。他们是我们的朋友泰德和凯瑟琳,我们是善意的。"

"安妮? 杰克?"那男人嘘了一声,"你们不是安妮和杰克!你们太小了!"

"我们不小了,"安妮说,"我已经九岁了,杰克也十岁了。"

"但你们还是小孩子,"大胡子鄙夷地说,"杰克和安妮可都是英雄!"

"真的吗? 我不知道我们能不能算英雄,"安妮回答,"我们不过有时帮助梅林和莫根·拉菲做点事情罢了。"

"安妮,嘘!"杰克制止了她。他不太信任坐在宝座上的人,担心安妮说得太多。

但是安妮继续说道:"是梅林让我们今天来白云后面的地方的。他给我们留了一个写在石头上的便条。"

"啊……,"宝座上的人说,"这么说你们真的就是安妮和杰克。"他身体前倾,小声念道:

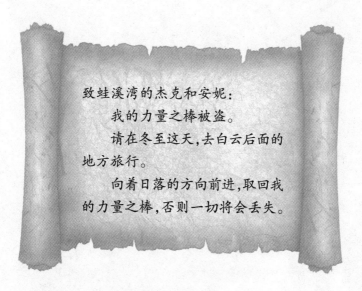

致蛙溪湾的杰克和安妮：

我的力量之棒被盗。

请在冬至这天，去白云后面的地方旅行。

向着日落的方向前进，取回我的力量之棒，否则一切将会丢失。

杰克不解，"你为什么……？"

"我为什么知道梅林的留言？"那人替杰克说完，"因为那个留言是我写的！我希望你们看到它。"

杰克不由得后退了一步。这么说梅林根本就没有给他们布置这个任务。是那个坐在宝座上的奇怪的男人欺骗了他们！

"你是谁？"泰德责问。

"我是寒冰巫师，"大胡子回答，"冬天的主宰。"

泰德深深地吸了一口气。

哦,不!杰克默念。在前几次的梅林任务中,他们就听说过这个巫师。就是他给乌鸦王下了咒语,并且还偷走了光明之剑!

巫师冷冷地盯着泰德和凯瑟琳。"你们俩是谁?"

"我是卡默洛特的泰德,"泰德回答,"我是莫根·拉菲的学徒,正在接受魔法师训练。"

"魔法师?"巫师质疑道。

"是的,"泰德说,"我爸爸是位魔法师,我妈妈是树精。"

"我是海豹,"凯瑟琳说,"我是远古的海豹种族的一员。"

"这么说你们都是来自我的世界,"冰雪巫师说,"那你们对于我来说就没有用了。"他转过头注视着杰克和安妮。"我只对这两个人类——来自蛙溪湾的杰克和安妮感兴趣。"

"你为什么对我们感兴趣?"杰克问。

"因为你们为梅林所做的一切!"冰雪巫师接着说,"你们帮他找到了记忆和想象之水!你们帮他找到了命运钻石!你们还帮他找到了光明之剑!现在我需要你们帮我也找一样东西。"

"你想要我们找什么？"安妮问。

冰雪巫师取下左眼上的眼罩，露出黑色、空洞的眼眶。

"噢！"安妮轻轻叫了一声。

"我需要你们去帮我找回我的眼睛！"冰雪巫师说。

"哦，天哪！"杰克惊呼。他有些害怕。

"你是认真的吗？"泰德问，"你要我们找回你的眼睛？"

巫师又把眼罩戴上。"是的，"他说，"我希望杰克和安妮帮我找到我的眼睛，把它带回来给我。"

"但是——为什么呢？"杰克问，"即使我们找到了你的眼睛，也没有用啊。我们不是医生。"

"而且，为什么你自己不去找回你的眼睛呢？"安妮接着问，"你是巫师啊！"

"不要违背我的命令！"巫师对安妮怒吼。

"喂！你不要对我妹妹大吼大叫！"杰克说。

巫师耸了耸他那浓密的眉毛。"你们是兄妹？"他问。

"不错！"杰克回答。

巫师缓缓地点点头，他的声音变得柔和起来，"你在保护你妹妹！"他说。

"我们互相保护！"杰克说。

"我明白了，"巫师轻声回答，然后他的声音又变得粗暴。"很久以前，我用我的眼睛去交换一件我非常想要的东西，但是我从没有得到那件东西。所以现在我想要回我的眼睛。"

"你是和谁交换的呢？"安妮问。

"命运三女神，"巫师回答，"我是和命运三女神交换的！但是她们骗了我！这就是我为什么需要你和杰克的帮助。你们必须去命运三女神那里找回我的眼睛，而且你们必须独自前往。"

"为什么要独自前往？"杰克问。

"因为只有人类才可以和命运三女神做交易，"冰雪巫师说，"像我这样的巫师不行，像你们的朋友那样的海豹女孩儿或者魔法师的儿子也不行。"

"但是在我们成功完成的其他任务里，泰德、凯瑟琳、莫根、还有梅林都帮助过我们！"安妮说。

"他们给过你们什么样的帮助呢？"巫师问。

"嗯，大部分都是咒语和谜语。"安妮回答。

"哦，这些我也可以做。"巫师说。他想了一会儿，然后身体前倾，用低沉的声音念道：

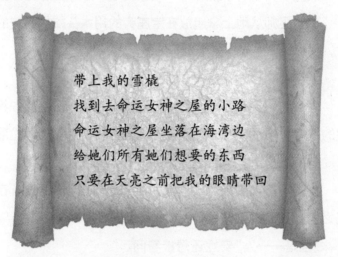

> 带上我的雪橇
> 找到去命运女神之屋的小路
> 命运女神之屋坐落在海湾边
> 给她们所有她们想要的东西
> 只要在天亮之前把我的眼睛带回

巫师把手伸进破旧长袍的口袋里，拿出一条打着结的厚实的绳子。"这条风绳能帮助你们在旅途中加快速度。"他说着把绳子丢给杰克。

风绳是什么东西？杰克心想，命运女神又是谁？

杰克正准备开口询问，冰雪巫师指着他说："现在听仔细这些警告：小心夜晚的狼。它们可能会在旅途中跟踪你们。千万别让它们追上。一旦被它们追上，你们的小命就玩儿完了！"

神奇树屋

MAGIC TREE HOUSE

杰克听得毛骨悚然。

冰雪巫师从地上拿起放在宝座旁的用木头雕刻而成的手杖，手杖润泽的光芒在月光下闪烁。

泰德惊呼："这是梅林的力量之棒！"

"不错，"巫师回答，他转向杰克和安妮，"现在就去找回我的眼睛吧，否则你们永远都别想再见到梅林和莫根·拉菲。"

"你对他们做了什么？"安妮质问。

巫师冷冷地看着她说："我不会告诉你的。你们只有在天亮之前找回我的眼睛，才可以看到他们。"

"但是——？"安妮还想接着问。

"不要再问了！"巫师打断了她，"出发吧！"几个孩子还没来得及说话，冰雪巫师就用梅林的力量之棒在空中一划，同时念道——"噢—奈！"

魔棒的末端闪出蓝色的火焰。片刻工夫，杰克、安妮、泰德和凯瑟琳就发现他们已经置身于宫殿外面寒冷的夜色中了。

带上我的雪橇

Take My Sleigh

　　巫师的雪橇飞快地在冰上滑行，把两只白狼远远地甩在后面。白狼的嗷叫声越来越弱，最后完全听不见了。

杰克坐在冰冷的地面上。安妮、泰德和凯瑟琳紧挨在一起。他们都震惊得说不出话来。夜很安静，一轮圆月在头顶闪闪发光，几颗星星在晴朗的夜空闪烁。

　　安妮首先打破了沉静。"我在想他对梅林和莫根做了什么！"她说。

　　"我在想你们应该去哪儿寻找他的眼睛。"泰德说。

　　"我在想我们用什么办法可以把他的眼睛带回。"杰克说。

　　"而我在担心狼是否就在附近！"凯瑟琳说。她站起来，环视了一下周围，把身上的斗篷又紧了紧。

　　"有谁记得冰雪巫师的咒语吗？"泰德问。

　　"我！"凯瑟琳回答。她把咒语一字不漏地重复了一遍：

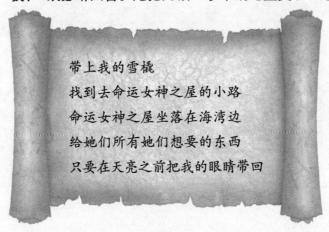

带上我的雪橇
找到去命运女神之屋的小路
命运女神之屋坐落在海湾边
给她们所有她们想要的东西
只要在天亮之前把我的眼睛带回

"命运女神是谁？"杰克问道。

"我在莫根的书里读到过关于命运女神的介绍，"泰德说，"据说命运女神是三姐妹，她们整天编织挂毯，她们编织的东西决定了所有居住在白云后面的人的命运。"

"这么说命运女神自己也长着眼睛？"杰克问，"跟冰雪巫师做交易的就是她们吗？"

"应该是的！"泰德说。

"他说我们必须带上他的雪橇去找命运女神，"安妮说。"那他的雪橇在哪儿呢？"

"瞧！"凯瑟琳往边上一指，"在那儿呢！"

"哦，对！"安妮说。

不远的地方，一艘外形奇特的银色雪橇无声地从雪堆后向他们滑过来，看上去就像一艘小小的有冰刀的帆船。没有人引导它，也没有马或者驯鹿拉动。桅杆上，一袭白帆静静地悬在空中。

雪橇停了下来。一声怪诞的嚎叫打破了这无风的夜的宁静。

"狼！"泰德惊呼，"我们要快点！"

凯瑟琳抓住他的胳膊说："别跑，如果我们乱跑，狼就会追赶我们。"

"噢，那当然，"泰德说，"不能让它们看出我们害怕。"

又一声嚎叫划破夜空。

"跑吧！"泰德喊了出来。

孩子们冲向雪橇，争着爬了进去。杰克和凯瑟琳站在前面，安妮和泰德站在后面。

"狼在那儿！"泰德一边惊呼，一边指向远处。"是白狼！"

杰克转过头，看见两只巨大的白狼在月光下的雪原奔驰。它们一边向雪橇狂奔，一边用大爪子扑落身上的雪花。

"走啊！快走啊！"杰克大叫，同时抓紧了雪橇的前端。

但是雪橇一动不动，而白狼离他们越来越近了。"到底怎样才能让雪橇动起来啊？"杰克问。

"用风绳！"泰德提醒。

杰克从口袋里拿出巫师给他的打了结的绳子。"怎么用呢？"杰克高喊。

"解开一个结！"泰德说。

杰克摘下手套。他试着解开一个绳结，可是他的手指不住地颤抖。这太离谱了！他想。解开一个结能有什么用呢？但是很快他解开了一个结。

一阵寒冷的微风从雪橇的后面吹来，吹动了头顶上的帆。

"再解开一个！"泰德喊道，"快！"

杰克很快又解开了一个。风变大了，帆又鼓起来了一些。雪橇的冰刀开始在雪上滑动。

　　"耶！"安妮欢呼，"雪橇开始动了！"

　　"是的，但是还不够快！"泰德说。

　　杰克回头看时，那两只白狼就快要追上他们了。它们在雪橇后面一边尖叫，一边狂奔，张大的嘴巴里尖利的牙齿闪着寒光。

　　杰克很快又解开了第三个结。冷风吹起白帆，只听"嘣"的一声，雪橇像离弦的箭一样向前冲去！

　　"站好！"泰德喊道。

　　杰克、安妮和凯瑟琳紧紧抓着雪橇的边沿，以免摔倒。泰德掌舵，驾驶着雪橇离开了冰宫。

　　巫师的雪橇飞快地在冰上滑行，把两只白狼远远地甩在后面。白狼的嗷叫声越来越弱，最后完全听不见了。

　　风继续推着银色的雪橇在冰雪中前进。冰刀在月光照耀的雪原上滑行，发出沙沙的声音。方形的白帆在风中翻腾，就像海盗船的风帆一样。甩掉了白狼，孩子们觉得坐雪橇其实很有趣，就是有些冷。

"你怎么知道解开绳子上的结就可以让风吹起来？"杰克问泰德。

"这是一个古老的魔法，"泰德解释道，"我在书里读到过风绳，但从来没见过。"

"你读过那么多书，真好！"安妮赞叹道。

"哦，快看！"凯瑟琳说，"野兔和狐狸！"

"在哪儿？"安妮问。

"在那儿！"凯瑟琳指向黑暗的远方，"它们正在雪地里玩儿呢！快听！在那片云朵的后面有天鹅呼啸而过。"

"哇！"安妮惊叹。

杰克被凯瑟琳超凡的听觉和视觉所折服。在这之前，这片月光照耀的平原对他来说是完全空旷的。

"你要把我们带到哪儿去？"安妮问泰德。

"我也不知道！"泰德笑着回答。

"我们应该去海湾边找命运女神的！"安妮说。

"那我们就向左转，跟着那些天鹅吧！"凯瑟琳说着指向雪原，"它们在向海边飞去。"

泰德把雪橇向左转。雪橇在雪上蹦上蹦下，过了一会儿，又平稳前进了。

"我们现在是在海面上!"凯瑟琳说,"下面有海豹,我可以看见它们呼吸的洞!我们是不是该停下来了?"

"的确!"泰德说,雪橇呼呼地继续在雪地上奔驰。"但是怎样停下来呢?"

"试着系上一个结!"安妮建议。

"好主意!"泰德说道,"杰克?"

杰克摘下手套,用颤抖、冰冷的双手在绳子上系了一个结。风变小了一些,雪橇的速度开始慢了下来。他又系了一个结,帆开始下垂。

"哦耶!"安妮欢呼。

在杰克系了第三个结以后,风完全消失了。雪橇缓缓停了下来。

"干得不错!"泰德赞道。

"谢谢,"杰克说,他把绳子收好放回口袋里,环顾四周。"这里就是命运女神仕的地方吗?"

"我去问问!"凯瑟琳说。

问谁呢?杰克想。

凯瑟琳爬出雪橇。她走在结冰的海面上，仔细观察，后来停在一个小洞旁边。

凯瑟琳跪了下来，轻柔地说着海豹语。她把耳朵贴在小洞上，仔细倾听。

过了一会儿，她站了起来。"海豹告诉我海湾边缘就在那些海边岩石的旁边，"她一边指一边说，"在那儿我们就可以找到命运女神了。"

"太棒了！"安妮说。

杰克、安妮、泰德和凯瑟琳在明亮的月光下越过冰冷的大海。他们在岩石间狭窄的通道里穿行。终于，他们走出了通道，停了下来。

"我们到了！"泰德说。

大约五十码外有一个白色的大土堆，土堆顶上的烟囱里有烟冒出来，圆形的小窗口闪着灯笼的微光。

"我知道你们必须独自为巫师的眼睛讨价还价，"泰德说，"但是我还是想看一眼这个土堆。"

他悄悄走到窗户边，向屋内看去。其他人跟在他身后。壁炉里的火烧得正旺。暗红的火光下，三个奇怪的生物在一台巨大的织布机前织布。杰克屏住了呼吸——那几个怪物的外貌太吓人了。

命运三女神瘦得如同骷髅一般。她们长着蓬乱的头发，长长的鼻子，巨大的、凸起的眼睛。她们弯曲、干瘦的手指在一幅巨大的挂毯上舞动。整个房间里，到处堆放着挂毯，直到屋顶。

"她们像童话故事里的巫婆！"安妮小声说。

"嗯，但她们不是巫婆，"泰德说，"她们编织的每一块布料都是真实的历史。"

"哇！"安妮惊叹。

"祝你们好运，"泰德说，"你们进去找巫师的眼睛，我和凯瑟琳就在外面等你们。"

突然，一声可怕的嚎叫划破了夜的宁静。

"呀！"安妮叫了出来。

"是白狼！"凯瑟琳说。

泰德快速移到门边，撞开门，说："大家都进来！"

于是他们四个人都挤进了命运女神的小屋。

命运女神

The Norns

　　三姐妹对她们的访客微微一笑。她们在织布机上跳动的、干瘦的手指就像在花朵上飞舞的蝴蝶。

泰德重重地关上门，把白狼关在外面。杰克屏住了呼吸。

"欢迎！"命运三女神齐声说。她们看上去很相像，只是穿着不同颜色的长袍，有蓝色、棕色和灰色。

"你们好吗，杰克、安妮、泰德、凯瑟琳？"穿蓝色袍子的命运女神说。

"我们很好！"安妮回答。

杰克很惊讶，命运女神怎么会知道他们的名字？她们虽然长相奇特，但是脸上挂着友善的微笑，眼睛亮闪闪的，这让杰克放松下来。在命运女神舒适的房间里，他从离家后第一次感到温暖。

"你们的旅途还顺利吗？"穿灰色袍子的命运女神问。

"还好，我们是坐冰雪巫师的雪橇来的！"安妮回答。

"还有风绳的帮助。"泰德补充道。杰克拿出绳子给三位女神看。

穿灰袍子的命运女神笑了，"是的，我们知道！我喜欢有结的绳子。"

"没有结的绳子太单调了！"穿蓝袍子的命运女神说。

"没有坎坷的人生也很单调！"穿棕色袍子的命运女神补

充道。

　　她们说话的时候也没有停止编织，突出的眼睛眨都不眨。杰克觉得她们好像从来都没有闭上过眼睛或者停止工作。

　　"不好意思打扰你们，"安妮说，"但是我和杰克只有找到冰雪巫师的眼睛，才能拯救我们的朋友梅林和莫根。"

　　"我们知道，"穿蓝袍子的命运女神说，"我们正在编织冰雪巫师的故事。过来看看吧。"

　　杰克和其他人一起走到织布机旁。正在织的这幅挂毯上有几十幅小的图画，所有的线用的都是冬天的颜色：蓝的、灰的、棕色的。

　　"这些图画描述了巫师过去的生活！"穿棕色袍子的命运女神解释说。

　　有一幅画上，两个孩子在一起玩耍。另一幅是一个男孩子在追赶天鹅。还有一幅是两只白狼。还有一幅是一只圆圈里的眼睛。

　　"关于这只眼睛有什么故事吗？"杰克问。

　　"很久以前，冰雪巫师来我们这儿寻找世界上所有的智慧，"穿灰袍子的巫师说，"我们说我们能给他智慧，只要他给我们他的一只眼睛。他同意了。"

"可是冰雪巫师看上去不是很有智慧呀！"安妮说。

"他的智慧确实不多，"穿棕色袍子的命运女神说，"我们在他的心里种下了智慧的种子，但是它们从未发芽。"

"你们为什么需要他的眼睛呢？"杰克问。

"我们想把它给冰冻巨人。"穿蓝袍子的命运女神说。

"冰冻巨人？"泰德不解，"谁是冰冻巨人？"

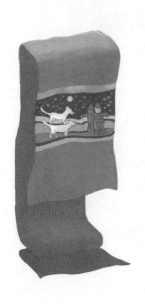

"他既不是魔法师，也不是人类，"穿蓝袍子的命运女神说，"他是大自然的黑暗势力，所经之处不会留下任何东西。"

"我们希望冰冻巨人可以用巫师的眼睛去看看这个美丽的世界，然后开始关心这个世界而不是毁灭它，"穿棕色袍子的命运女神说，"但是，唉！冰冻巨人根本没有用过我们给他的礼物，反而一直把它藏在我们给他时最初放置的地方。"

"那个地方在哪儿？"安妮问。

"冰冻巨人睡觉的空空山。"穿灰袍子的命运女神说。

"空空山有一个山洞。"穿蓝袍子的命运女神说。

"山洞里有一块冰雹。"穿棕色袍子的命运女神说。

"冰雪巫师的眼睛就藏在冰雹的正中间。"穿灰袍子的命运女神接着说。

杰克闭上眼睛重复道：

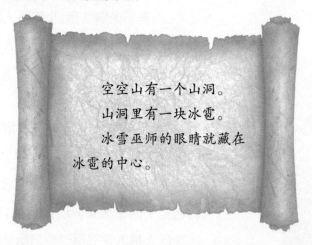

空空山有一个山洞。
山洞里有一块冰雹。
冰雪巫师的眼睛就藏在冰雹的中心。

"对！"穿灰袍子的命运女神说，"那就是你们要去的地方。但是要记住：千万不要直视冰冻巨人。任何直视冰冻巨

人的人都会在顷刻
之间冻死。"

　　杰克颤抖着点了
点头。

　　"那我们现在就出
发吧，"安妮说，"谢谢你们的帮助。冰雪巫师在咒语里告诉
我们给你们任何你们想要的东西。"

　　命运女神相互看了看。"我喜欢围在你脖子上的编织物，"
穿灰袍子的命运女神对她的姐妹说，"它的红色就像火红的霞
光。"另外两位命运女神渴望地点了点头。

　　"我的围巾？"安妮说，"没问题，给您吧！"她取下自己
红色的羊绒围巾，放在离命运女神织布机很近的地方。

　　"真好看！"穿蓝袍子的命运女神赞道，"也许我们应该
停止编织命运，改为编织围巾了！"

　　另一个命运女神哈哈地笑了。"出发吧！"穿灰袍子的命
运女神说，"向着北极星的方向前进。到达雪山以后，记住找

一座没有顶端的山头。"

杰克、安妮和泰德起身向门口走去，只有凯瑟琳留在后面。"不好意思，我还有一个问题，"她说。她指着画有天鹅和男孩儿的那幅画问："这幅画讲的是什么故事呢？"

"这是一个悲伤的故事，"穿灰袍子的命运女神说，"冰雪巫师有一个妹妹，她爱巫师胜过世界上的一切事物。有一天他们因为很愚蠢的事情吵架了。巫师发了脾气，让他的妹妹永远离开他。妹妹哭着跑到海边，在那儿她碰到了一群天鹅少女。她们给了她一件白色羽毛裙子。她穿上裙子，变成一只天鹅，和其他的天鹅一起飞走了，再也没有回来。"

"在这之后，冰雪巫师变得和以前不一样了，"穿蓝袍子的命运女神说，"自他妹妹走了以后，冰雪

巫师变得冷淡而刻薄，就好像他的妹妹带走了他的心一样。"

"太可怜了，"安妮说，"那冰雪巫师的故事会有怎样的结局呢？"

"决定我们下一步将要编织什么的是你们，而不是我们！"穿棕色袍子的命运女神说。

"我们？"安妮问。

"是的，"穿灰袍子的命运女神说，"我们的力量正在消失，我们的计划不再按照我们的预期发展。冰雪巫师没有得到智慧！冰冻巨人也没有得到眼睛！你们必须马上出发，去完成这个故事。"

三姐妹对她们的访客微微一笑。她们在织布机上跳动的、干瘦的手指就像在花朵上飞舞的蝴蝶。

杰克也忍不住对她们笑了。但是当他想到梅林和莫根，他便又记起在外面等着他们的危险。"最后一个问题，"他说，"那两只白狼的故事是什么？"

"哦，白狼！"穿蓝袍子的命运女神说，"别害怕那些狼！

没有狼的世界是很枯燥的！"她的两个姐妹微笑着点头。在那一刻，她们的微笑让杰克不再害怕白狼、冰雪巫师和冰冻巨人。

孩子们挥手告别了命运三女神，离开小屋，回到外面寒冷的夜晚。

在空空山

In the Hollow Hill

　　银色的雪橇在大风雪中急行，杰克抱紧
自己以抵御寒冷。他一直在留心那两只白狼
的踪迹，但是他没有再看到它们。

站在寒冷中，杰克又感到害怕了。房子周围的雪地上有大大的爪印。

"白狼来过这儿！"凯瑟琳说。

"也许我们应该回到屋里。"泰德说。

"不，"凯瑟琳反对，"我们必须和杰克、安妮一起回到雪橇那儿，送他们去空空山。"

"哦，那当然！"泰德一边说一边点头。

他们小心翼翼地向岩石走去。杰克回头最后看了一眼命运女神的小屋，他希望他可以回到那个舒适温暖的地方。

凯瑟琳把手放在杰克的肩膀上说，"来，我们必须快点儿！"

孩子们又走上岩石间的通道。他们来到通道的尽头，没有发现白狼的踪影。银色的雪橇在月光下等着他们归来。杰克和安妮爬进雪橇。

"你们不能和我们一起去吗？"杰克问泰德和凯瑟琳，"我记得你说过如果我们在一起，可以完成任何任务。"

"是的，"泰德说，"但是冰雪巫师说过只有人类才可以和命运三女神做交易。"

"别害怕！"凯瑟琳说，"我们的心和你们同在，而且我们

会在黎明时分在巫师的宫殿和你们会合。"

"你们怎么去那儿呢?"安妮问。

"我可以试试几个咒语!"泰德笑着说。

"我也有一些海豹人的魔法!"凯瑟琳说。

"我们有风绳!"安妮说。

"赶快去空空山吧!"凯瑟琳说。

"记住命运女神的话,"泰德提醒,"不要直视冰冻巨人。"

"知道了!"杰克说。他拿出风绳,取下手套,解开一个结,风开始吹了。

杰克又解开一个结。风变大了,帆被鼓起,冰刀向前滑动。

杰克解开第三个结,风变得更大了,白帆高涨,雪橇在夜色中前行。

"保持速度!"泰德在后面大喊。

杰克和安妮跟他们挥手告别。雪橇在海面的冰块上迅速滑过,很快就跃上了白雪覆盖的平原,急速右转。

"不对,是向着北极星的方向!"杰克告诉安妮。

安妮掌舵,把雪橇调整到正确的方向。他们向远方闪亮的北极星驶去。

银色的雪橇在大风雪中急行,杰克抱紧自己以抵御寒冷。他一直在留心那两只白狼的踪迹,但是他没有再看到它们。

很快他就看见远方成排的白雪覆盖的山峦。"瞧!"他说,"在那儿!"他指的是那唯一的一座无头山。

"把雪橇停下来!"安妮喊道。

杰克系了一个结,雪橇慢了下来。他又系了两个结,风完全停了,雪橇在空空山的脚下停住了。杰克和安妮爬下雪橇。

杰克望着陡峭的白山坡,说道"我们怎么进去呢?"

"我也不知道,"安妮回答,"你说冰冻巨人是怎么进去的?"

　　"哦……冰冻巨人！"杰克说。他真希望泰德和凯瑟琳能够和他们一起来。现在他感觉就像是一个团队的一部分丢失了一样。

　　安妮好像读懂他了的心思。"我们可以完成任务的，"她说，"为了梅林和莫根我们必须完成任务。"

　　杰克点点头，"说得对。"他们在月光下仔细打量那座山。

　　"那上面是入口吗？"安妮问。

　　"也许吧，"杰克说，"我们爬上去看看。"他们往山上爬了一小段，杰克可以清晰地看到白雪覆盖的山坡上有一个裂痕。

　　"看看这道裂缝是不是通向山里！"安妮说。

　　"等等，如果冰冻巨人在里面怎么办？"杰克说。

　　"我觉得他现在不在里面，"安妮回答，"我们最好在他回来之前找到巫师的眼睛。"

"好的，"杰克说，"但是要小心。"

他们又沿着山坡往上爬了一段，来到一个洞口，从那个巨大的裂痕走了进去。

杰克和安妮发现他们置身于一个深陷的圆洞的边上，月光从山顶的洞口处照了进来。洞的底部有一个平整的圆圈，看上去就像是雪被一圈圈地吹了下来。

"这一定是巨人睡觉的地方！"安妮说。

"嗯，说不定就是他藏眼睛的地方，"杰克说，"我们需要找到一个洞，记得吗？"他重复着命运女神说过的话：

空空山有一个山洞。
山洞里有一块冰雹。
冰雪巫师的眼睛就藏
在冰雹的中心。

"对！"安妮说。

杰克探头去看下面的白雪的旋涡。他回视安妮，"下去吗？"

"下去吧！"安妮小声说。

杰克和安妮爬了下去。他们小心地穿过银色的月光，在地面上仔细寻找洞口。

安妮被什么东西绊倒。"哇！"她叫了一声，"我觉得我找到那个洞了！我刚刚踩进去了！"

"真的吗？"杰克问。他在她旁边跪下。

安妮把手伸进地面上的一个小洞里。"里面有东西！"她说，她掏出一块鸡蛋大小的冰块。"这就是冰雹！"

在朦胧的月光下，他们无法分辨冰块里是不是有东西。"不知道这是不是我们要找的冰雹，"杰克说，"我们要等到白天才能看清楚眼睛在不在里面。"

"这应该就是我们要找的，"安妮说，"你说这个空空山里总共能有多少块冰雹被藏在洞里？"

"有道理！"杰克说。

安妮把冰雹放在头顶。"也许这只眼睛正在看着我们！"她说。

"从科学的角度来说这是不可能的,"杰克说,"一只眼睛只有和大脑连在一起的时候才能看见东西。"

"是,从科学的角度绳子也不能让风吹起来,"安妮说,"在这里忘记科学吧。等等——"她忽然屏住了呼吸,"你感觉到了吗？"

"感觉到什么？"杰克问。

"地面在颤动！"安妮说。

杰克也感觉到大地的颤动了。他还听见一个奇怪的声音——巨大的呜呼声——从山外传来,呜呼呼,呜呼呼……听上去像是呼吸声。

"巨人回来了！"安妮说。

"哦,不！"杰克叫了起来。

大地还在颤动。呼吸声听上去更近了一些。

"把冰雹藏起来！"杰克说。

安妮把大冰块放到口袋里。

呜呼呼,呜呼呼,呜呼呼……巨人好像已经进来了！

"他来了！"安妮说。

"躲起来！"杰克小声说。

他把安妮推到阴暗处。他记得那个穿灰袍子的命运女神的警告：任何一个直视冰冻巨人的人都会立刻被冻死。

"不论你做什么，千万别看他！"杰克小声地叮嘱安妮。

他们隐藏在黑暗里，把脸埋在手中，等待着……

7

冰冻巨人

The Frost Giant

杰克发出一声轻叹。冰雹中的眼球正从里面凝视着他。那眼球有一块大理石那么大，外延是白色的，中间是亮蓝色。

呜呼呼，呜呼呼，呜呼呼……伴着冰冻巨人的一声声呼吸，一股寒流席卷了整个山洞。

杰克颤抖着，感觉寒气刺骨。呜呼呼，呜呼呼，呜呼呼……

巨人的呼吸变得越来越响。杰克紧闭双眼，任寒冷潮湿的风吹打着他的身体。

呜呼呼，呜呼呼，呜呼呼……

杰克把身体埋得更低一些，紧靠着安妮。

呜呼呼，呜呼呼，呜呼呼……

巨人的呼吸就好像上百个鬼怪在洞里嚎叫。杰克想起那个穿蓝色袍子的命运女神的话：他是大自然的黑暗势力，他会摧毁任何挡住他去路的东西。

但是突然，巨人的呼吸变得轻柔了。发生什么事儿了？杰克有些好奇。

呼吸声变得越来越小。"也许他快睡着了！"安妮悄悄地说。

呼吸变得平静而稳定，犹如微风拂过一般。

"这下应该是睡着了，"安妮小声说，"咱们趁机溜出去吧。"

"好的，但是眼睛要一直往下看，只能看着地面！"杰克小

声叮嘱。

"好！"安妮回答。

他们低着头，小心翼翼地穿过山洞，向洞口爬去。杰克的牙齿在打颤，他不能分辨是因为寒冷还是因为害怕。

突然，一声震耳欲聋的咆哮震撼了夜空！冰冻巨人的尖叫带来了愤怒的风暴。他醒了！

杰克被吹倒在地。他很想爬过雪地，但是他不知道该往哪边爬，而且他不敢抬头看。

"杰克！这边！"安妮的声音盖过了巨人的咆哮。她帮助杰克站了起来，两人挣扎着和狂风抗争，终于来到了洞口。

他们迅速爬出山洞。外面的狂风几乎要把他们吹倒。他们挣扎着爬下山。

风卷起雪花在平原上旋转。"安妮！安妮！"杰克大喊。她在哪儿？雪橇在哪儿？他什么也看不见。他甚至站都站不稳。

风更大了。一大堆雪块从山上滚下来，触地时破碎成大团白色的粉末。

"杰克！杰克！"

杰克听见安妮的声音从呼啸的寒风中传来。他想试着站起来，但是雪不断地砸在他身上，直到把他完全掩埋。

杰克被埋在雪里，身体渐渐失去了所有的力气。他知道他应该挖出一条路，但是他实在太冷太累了。他累得没有力气去找安妮，没有力气去和冰冻巨人搏斗。他闭上眼睛，在寒冷中渐渐昏睡了过去。

杰克梦见冰冷的毛皮拍打着他的脸。他梦见一只狼在他身边刨雪，在推他，在拉他，还用鼻子嗅他……

杰克睁开眼睛，觉得一阵眩晕。一开始他什么也看不见，但是他能感觉到自己不是被埋在雪下。他擦了擦眼镜，看见月亮和星星低低地挂在晴朗的夜空。

冰冻巨人一定已经离开了，杰克心想。过了一会儿，他听到气喘吁吁的声音。他站起来，环顾四周。一只白狼正蹲在他后面！

杰克挣扎了几步。"走开！"他大叫。

白狼嗥叫着退后了几步。

"滚！滚！滚开！"杰克继续大喊。他抓起雪球向白狼砸过去。

白狼又退后了几步。杰克环视四周,发现安妮躺在雪地上一动不动,另一只白狼在她身边嗅着,不住地拍打她。

　　愤怒让杰克变得无畏。"别碰她!"他高喊,"滚开!"他抓起更多的雪球向白狼扔过去。

　　白狼退后了一些。

　　"滚!滚!"杰克怒吼,"走开!别碰我们!"他愤怒地注视着那两只白狼。

　　白狼回视杰克,黄色的眼睛闪着凶光。

　　"我不是开玩笑——滚开!"杰克尖叫。

　　他恶狠狠地怒视两只白狼。终于,白狼移开了视线。它们相互对视了一下,慢慢地后退。它们最后扫了杰克和安妮一眼,转身小跑着离开了。

　　杰克冲向安妮,跪在她身边,扶起她的头。"醒醒!快醒醒!"他说。安妮睁开了眼睛。

　　"你没事儿吧?"杰克问。

　　"没事儿……我梦见白狼了!"安妮咕哝了一句。

　　"我也是!"杰克说,"等我醒过来,它们真的就在这儿!它们还差点儿吃了我们!""真的吗?"安妮坐起来,环视四周。

"真的,但是我把它们吓跑了!"杰克说。

"那冰冻巨人呢?"安妮问。

"他也走了,"杰克说,"来,我们离开这儿!"他扶着安妮站起来。"巫师的眼睛还在你那儿吧?"

安妮摸了摸口袋,"在!"她回答。

"好。"杰克看了看周围。在一堆堆落下来的雪块旁边,他们的雪橇在静静地等着他们。头顶上的天空已经变成了亮灰色。

"快天亮了,"杰克说,"还记得巫师说的话吗?我们要在天亮之前把他的眼睛带回去,否则我们就再也见不到莫根和梅林了!"

他握住安妮的手,两人一起在雪地里穿行。他们走到雪橇边,爬了进去。安妮掌舵,杰克取出风绳,解开一个结。

微风吹向雪橇。杰克解开第二个结,帆被充起。他解开第三个结,银色雪橇开始前进,滑过白色的平原。

沙——沙——沙。雪橇滑过厚厚的积雪,把空空山远远抛在身后。当他们越过白色的平原时,天空从灰色变成了淡粉色。

"我们得快点儿！"安妮说。

杰克解开了第四个结。风在他们的耳边呼啸，雪橇加快了速度。安妮驾驶着雪橇穿过岩石，越过海面，跨过平原，向冰雪巫师的宫殿驶去。

当雪橇接近宫殿时，杰克系上一个结，雪橇慢了下来。他接着又系了三个结，雪橇完全停住了。

杰克和安妮借着微弱寒冷的光芒环顾四周。"我在想泰德和凯瑟琳在哪儿，"安妮说，"他们说过会在黎明前在这里等我们的。"

杰克用目光搜寻着巨大的白色平原，但是没有看到他们朋友的影子。他真希望他能有凯瑟琳的视力。"希望他们平安无事，"他说，"希望他们没有碰到白狼。"

"我觉得白狼不会伤害他们，"安妮说，"我梦见的白狼看上去很善良。"

"我梦见的白狼也跟真的不同！"杰克说。

"我觉得我们不能再等了，"安妮说，"眼睛要赶在太阳升起之前送到冰雪巫师那里。"

"眼睛！"杰克一惊，"我们还没有确认眼睛是不是在冰雹

里呢。"

安妮从口袋里拿出冰雹，把它举起。

杰克发出一声轻叹。冰雹中的眼球正从里面凝视着他。那眼球有一块大理石那么大，外延是白色的，中间是亮蓝色。

"哦，天哪！"杰克惊叹。

"真漂亮啊，对吧？"安妮说。

"我不知道！"杰克有些不太确定。一只不在人脑袋上的眼睛看上去总归有些奇怪。"把它收起来吧！"他说。

安妮把冰雹放回口袋。杰克再次环顾四周。天空已经从淡粉色变成红色，地平线上显现出太阳的浅银色光芒。

"太阳！"杰克惊叫，"快！"他和安妮跳下雪橇，向宫殿跑去。

当他们来到宫殿门口时，安妮停了下来。"瞧！"她指着雪地上的大爪印说，"狼的脚印。"

"哦，不！"杰克喊了一声，"难道那两只白狼在里面吗？这太奇怪了。"

"没关系！我们必须进去！快！"安妮说。就在火红的太阳跃出地平线的一刹那，他们冲进了宫殿。

找回眼睛

Return of the Eye

　　巫师小心翼翼地撬开碎片,取出眼睛。他把眼睛高高举起,仔细打量。然后,伴随一声渴望的哭喊,他摘下了眼罩。

杰克和安妮穿过宫殿的前厅,绕过冰柱,来到巫师宝座所在的房间。地面和墙壁在黎明寒冷而烂漫的晨光下闪烁。

"呜——哦。"杰克喊了一声。

巫师正在等他们,而那两只白狼分别卧在宝座的两侧睡觉。杰克困惑了:它们怎么在这儿? 难道它们是属于巫师的吗?

白狼抬起头,嗅了嗅空气,耳朵竖了起来。当它们看见杰克和安妮,立刻站了起来,尖利的黄眼睛紧盯着他们。

冰雪巫师也紧紧盯着杰克和安妮。"怎么样? "他问,"你们把我的眼睛带回来了吗? "

"带回来了!"杰克回答。

安妮从口袋里拿出冰雹,把它递给巫师。冰雹从安妮的小手传到巫师粗糙的大手里,而杰克在一旁一直紧张地盯着那两只白狼。

巫师低下头看了看冰块,又抬眼看向杰克和安妮。"你们不愧是英雄! "他冷冷地说。

"算不上了。"杰克嘟哝了一句。

巫师审视着冰雹中的眼睛。突然,他抓起冰雹朝宝座的把手猛力地撞去。

杰克和安妮屏住呼吸后退了一步。巫师再次抓住冰雹砸向宝座的把手。这一次,冰雹碎了。

巫师小心翼翼地撬开碎片,取出眼睛。他把眼睛高高举起,仔细打量。然后,伴随一声渴望的哭喊,他摘下了眼罩。

杰克和安妮颇有兴致地看着巫师把眼睛放进自己漆黑空洞的眼眶。杰克屏住了呼吸,他觉得又可怕又有趣。他不相信一个人可以这样把眼睛安回脑袋里。

巫师慢慢地低下头,好像停止了呼吸。他有两只眼睛了,但是这只新的眼睛并不转动,好像还在冰封的状态。

杰克开始担心。如果巫师的眼睛仍然看不见,那他可能就不会帮助他们了。"我们把你的眼睛带回来了,"他说,"你现在可以告诉我们莫根和梅林在哪儿了吧?"

巫师抬起头看着杰克。他用一只手盖住一只眼睛,然后再盖住另一只。过了一会儿,他又重复了几次,盖住又放开眼睛。

终于,巫师放下手,喊道:"不!"他的吼叫震动了冰柱。"你们欺骗了我!"

"不,我们没有!"安妮说。

"这只眼睛没有用！"巫师嚷道，"它是死的！看不见东西！"

"但这就是你给命运女神的眼睛啊！"安妮说，"你还保证过，如果我们把它带回来，你就把梅林和莫根还给我们。"

两只白狼仰头长啸。

"不！"巫师大叫，"你们欺骗了我！你们欺骗了我！"

"我们还是离开这里吧！"杰克悄悄地说。他拉着安妮向冰柱走去。

"站住！"巫师怒吼，"你们逃不出我的手掌心！"他拿起梅林的力量之棒。白狼仕一旁咆哮。巫师用魔杖指着杰克和安妮。他开始念咒语："罗——

伊——"

"等等!"有人在呼喊。泰德冲了进来。"等等!"

巫师的魔杖停在了空中,他疯狂地盯着泰德,他的脸因为愤怒而扭曲。

"我们有东西要给你!"泰德对巫师喊道。"凯瑟琳!"他回头轻唤。

凯瑟琳从柱子后面走了出来,跟她一起的还有一位留着长辫子的女孩儿。她的肩膀上披着白色羽毛做的斗篷,她的目光停留在巫师身上,明亮的微笑在她的脸庞绽开。她慢慢地向宝座走去。

巫师放下梅林的魔棒。他出神地看着这位年轻的女子。他脸上所有的颜色都褪去了。有一会儿,他就像雕像一样一动不动。良久,一滴蓝色的、冰冷的眼泪从他冰冻的眼睛里流了出来,流过他苍白的脸颊。

杰克、安妮、泰德和凯瑟琳站在一旁,看着年轻的女子和巫师静静地望着对方。

"那是他妹妹天鹅小姐吗?"安妮小声问。

"是!"凯瑟琳小声回答。

天鹅小姐用奇怪的语言对冰雪巫师说："VAL-EE-VEN-O-WAN。"

巫师没有回答，但是泪水从他的两只眼睛里溢出。

"VAL-EE-VEN-O-WAN。"天鹅小姐又说了一遍。

"她在说什么？"杰克问。

"她在说，我回来原谅你了！"凯瑟琳解释道。

巫师站了起来。他走下宝座，轻柔地抚摸天鹅小姐的脸庞，就像是确认这是不是真的一样。然后他温柔地回答："FEL-O-WAN。"

"你们是怎么找到她的？"杰克问泰德。

"一只海豹带着我们从冰面下去，到了天鹅的小岛！"泰德说。

"我们找到她以后，就告诉她巫师是多么地思念她，"凯瑟琳接着说，"我还告诉她你们俩的故事，还有你们是怎样互相帮助的。我劝她回到哥哥身边，重归于好。"

巫师和他妹妹一直在用奇怪的语言轻声交谈。温暖的阳光透过宫殿的窗户照了进来。

安妮上前一步。"嗯，打扰一下！"她说。

巫师看着她。"我妹妹已经回来了，"他惊喜地说，"现在我的两个眼睛也都可以看见了。我看得非常清楚。"

"我很高兴，"安妮说，"但是你必须把梅林和莫根还给我们。"

巫师看着他的妹妹，她点了点头。巫师拿出梅林的力量之棒。"用这个把他们唤回来吧，"他说，"握紧力量之棒，然后呼唤他们。"他把魔棒交给安妮。

安妮的手勉强能握住魔棒。"跟我一起握住它，杰克！"她说。

杰克上前，帮助安妮握住魔棒。金色、光滑的力量之棒在手中感觉温暖而有活力。

兄妹俩一起握住魔棒，安妮呼唤着："梅林、莫根，回来吧！"

魔棒的末端冒出一股蓝色的亮光，射向那两只白狼。

突然，狼的眼睛变成了人的眼睛！狼鼻子变成了人鼻子！狼嘴巴变成了人嘴巴！狼耳朵变成了人的耳朵！狼爪子变成了人的手和脚！狼的皮毛变成了红色的长斗篷！

两只狼不见了，一个男人和一个女人出现在他们面前。

心灵的智慧

Wisdom of the Heart

　　现在,世界对于杰克来说一点儿都不可怕
了。所有的事物都明亮而平静。温和的、玫瑰
色的阳光穿过了清晨的云朵。

"梅林！莫根！"安妮欢呼道。

　　泰德和凯瑟琳喜极而泣。

　　安妮冲向莫根抱住了她。

　　杰克觉得一身轻松。"您好！"他说，"您好！"

　　"欢迎回来，先生！"泰德对梅林说。

　　"谢谢，"梅林回答，他看着杰克和安妮，"谢谢你们帮我们变回了自己。"

　　"我们不知道白狼就是你和莫根！"安妮说。

　　"我们跟着你们是为了帮助你们！"莫根说。

　　"巫师告诉我们如果让你们抓住了，就会被吃掉！"杰克说。

　　"是吗？"莫根问。

　　他们都看着冰雪巫师。他和他的妹妹站在一起，愧疚地看着莫根和梅林。

　　"我害怕他们和你们靠得太近了会认出你们，"他说，"但是我不会再做任何对你们不利的事情了，我发誓——因为我现在可以看得很清楚了。"巫师回头看着他的妹妹，蓝色的眼睛里闪着快乐的光芒。

　　"你现在可以看见是因为你已经找回了你的心，"莫根说，

"你丢失的不光是你的眼睛,还有你的心。我们是用眼睛和心灵一起看世界的。"

"而且现在也许你还能找回你向命运女神索要的智慧,"梅林说,"智慧是用心灵和大脑一起获得的。"

冰雪巫师点了点头。"请用你们的心来原谅我," 他说,"让我的雪橇把你们安全地送回家吧!"

"好的,我们现在确实得离开了,"莫根说,"我们已经离开卡默洛特太久了。"

"下次你再来卡默洛特的时候,我的朋友,我们会像对待客人一样招待你,"梅林说,"不要再像小偷一样在晚上悄悄地来了。"

"还要记得带上你的妹妹。"莫根说。

"我一定会的!"巫师回答。

梅林看着杰克、安妮、泰德和凯瑟琳,问:"准备好出发了吗?"

"好了,先生!"他们齐声答道。

梅林看着杰克手中的力量之棒。

"哦!对不起,我差点儿忘了。"杰克说。他把沉重的魔棒交还给梅林。

梅林握住魔棒，看上去顿时能量大增。"我们走吧！"他轻快地说。

梅林和莫根带着大家走出房间，红色的斗篷在他们身后飞舞。泰德和凯瑟琳紧紧跟随，杰克和安妮也跟在他们后面。

在他们快要离开房间时，杰克和安妮再次回头看了看冰雪巫师和他的妹妹。他们又深深地陷入交谈中。

"他们有好几年没有看到对方了，"安妮说，"他们一定有很多话要说。"

"是的，"杰克说，他不能想象好几年看不到安妮。"来吧，我们走。"他握住安妮的手，拉着她走出房间，穿过前厅，走进寒冷的黎明。

杰克和安妮跟着他们的四位卡默洛特的朋友来到雪橇边。大家一个接一个地爬上雪橇。

安妮掌舵，杰克站在前面。他拿出风绳，解开一个结。雪橇晃了晃。他又解开一个结，雪橇开始缓缓前行。

雪橇比以前重了，所以杰克又快速地解开了两

个结。雪橇飞速地在雪地上穿行。

"保持速度！"泰德说。

雪橇在黎明中滑行。安妮转过头问莫根和梅林："你们可以告诉我冰冻巨人长得什么样子吗？"

梅林笑着说："根本就没有什么冰冻巨人。"

"什么？"凯瑟琳和泰德一起说。

"一定有的，"安妮说，"我们听见了他的呼吸。"

"他差点儿就把我们冻死了！"杰克说。

"晚上，风通常是呈环形在空空山旋转的，"梅林说，"你们就经历了一次这样的风暴。"

"那么命运女神讲的把巫师的眼睛给冰冻巨人的故事呢？"杰克问。

"很多古时候的人认为大自然的力量掌握在一个实实在在的巨人或怪物手里，"莫根解释说，"命运女神是最后一代这样的人。她们认为冰冻巨人是一个住在空空山的活生生的生灵，但实际上冰冻巨人从来没有接受过她们的礼物，因为根本就没有什么冰冻巨人。"

杰克摇摇头。"我们当时还相信了命运女神说的话。她们告诉我们如果我们直视冰冻巨人就会被冻死。"

"而且我们也相信了冰雪巫师的话，"安妮说，"他告诉我们如果被狼抓住了就会被吃掉。"

"人们总是试图让我们相信世界比它的真实面目要可怕！"莫根说。

现在，世界对于杰克来说一点儿都不可怕了。所有的事物都明亮而平静。温和的、玫瑰色的阳光穿过了清晨的云朵。

"今天是冬至后的第一天，"莫根说，"从今天起光明会回来，白天会变长。"

杰克转向太阳的方向，他看见树屋就停在不远处的雪堆上。

杰克系上了风绳上的一个结。他又接着系了三个结，雪橇在雪堆旁停了下来。

梅林看着他们，"在冬至这天你们展现了超凡的勇气，你们经受住了大风暴和极度寒冷的考验，还帮助冰雪巫师和他的妹妹重归于好。也许最重要的是，你们帮我找回了力量之棒。我感谢你们！"

"不用谢！"杰克和安妮谦虚地说。

"你们在前四次任务中为卡默洛特王国做出了巨大的贡

献，"梅林继续说，"在你们的下一次历险中，你们会回到你们的现实世界，而不是魔法世界。"

"我们会很快再来看你们的！"莫根说。

"太棒了！"安妮说。

杰克和安妮从雪橇上爬下来。他们看着泰德和凯瑟琳说："希望在下一次的旅行中还能得到你们的帮助。"

泰德笑着回答："如果我们四个在一起，就可以完成任何任务，不是吗？"

"当然！"杰克和安妮齐声回答。然后，他们爬上了雪堆。到了雪堆顶上，他们从窗户爬进树屋，立刻转身往外看。

雪橇已经消失了。

"再见！"安妮轻轻地说。

杰克捡起地上的灰色小石块。他指着巫师留言中的蛙溪湾说："我希望我们可以去那里。"

风开始吹了。

风越刮越大。

然后一切都静止了。

完全静止。

* * *

杰克睁开眼睛。他们又回到了蛙溪湾的小树林。自从他们离开以后,时间一点都没有流逝。快到黄昏了,树屋外的雪花像小羽毛一般片片飘落。

　　安妮颤抖着说:"好冷。"

　　"来,围上我的围巾。"杰克说着摘下自己的围巾。

　　"不,你也需要的。"安妮拒绝了。

　　"还是你戴吧,我没事儿。"杰克把自己的围巾围在安妮的脖子上。"如果妈妈问你围巾,你怎么回答呢?"他问。

　　"我就告诉她,命运三女神把它要去了,作为告诉我们冰雪巫师的眼睛在空空山的山洞里的回报。"安妮回答。

　　"好吧!"杰克说着也笑了。

　　"我们最好在天黑之前赶回家。"安妮说。她爬下绳梯,杰克跟在后面。

　　他们来到地面,杰克忽然想起了风绳。"我们忘记把风绳还回去了,"他说着伸手从口袋里掏出风绳,"不过我想梅林的魔法能够驾驶雪橇回到卡默洛特。"

　　杰克和安妮看着风绳,"解开一个结。"安妮轻轻地说。

　　杰克取下手套,解开一个结。他屏住呼吸等待着。什么也没有发生。他朝安妮笑了笑,"我想,在我们的世界里,它

只是一根普通的绳子罢了。"

杰克把风绳放回口袋。他们在白雪覆盖的林间穿行。杰克一边走,一边寻找泰德和凯瑟琳的脚印,但是一个也没找到。

杰克和安妮走出树林,来到他们居住的街道。他们看见每一家的圣诞树和窗户里的烛火都在闪闪发光。

他们的靴子踩在白雪覆盖的地面上咯吱咯吱地响。兄妹俩走到门廊前的台阶时,杰克定住了。他吃惊地看到:

安妮的红色围巾就挂在门廊的栏杆上。

"我真不敢相信这是真的!"杰克说。

"我信!"安妮说。

他们跑上台阶,安妮一把抓住她的围巾:"瞧!"

她把围巾拿给杰克看。围巾上绣了一小幅画儿,一幅有安妮、杰克和两只白狼的画儿。

杰克无语。

"酷吧?"安妮说。她把杰克的围巾还给杰克,把自己的围巾围上,把有画儿的部分塞进外套里。

前门打开了,甜美的香味从屋子里飘散出来。

"回来了?"妈妈说,"饼干已经做好了,快进来暖和暖和吧!"

寒冰巫师

●《寒冰巫师》是梅林任务四部曲的结束。在这四个任务中，杰克和安妮为梅林找到了法宝——记忆和想象之锅中的水、命运钻石、光明之剑和法力魔杖。这四样东西都是受到"卡默洛特四宝贝"的启发想出来的。根据爱尔兰传说，它们是古代凯尔特人视为最神圣的四样东西。

寒冰巫师

WINTER OF THE ICE WIZARD

寒冰巫师

WINTER OF THE ICE WIZARD

CONTENTS

Winter Solstice

A cold wind rattled the windowpanes. But inside the house, it was warm and cozy. Jack and Annie were making Christmas cookies with their mom. Jack pressed a star—shaped cookie cutter into the dough.

"Hey, it's snowing outside," said Annie.

Jack looked out the window. Huge snowflakes were falling from the late-afternoon sky.

"You want to go out?" asked Annie.

"Not really. It'll be dark soon," said Jack.

"That's right," said their mom. "Today's the first day of winter. It's the shortest day of the year."

Jack's heart skipped a beat. "You mean it's the *winter solstice?*" he said.

"Yes," said their mom.

Annie gasped. "The winter solstice?" she said.

"Yes...," their mom said, puzzled.

Jack and Annie looked at each other. Last summer,

Merlin the magician had called for their help on the *summer* solstice. Maybe he would need them again today!

Jack put down the cookie cutter and wiped his hands on a towel. "Actually, Mom, it might be fun to play in the snow for just a few minutes," he said.

"Whatever you want," their mom said. "Just dress warmly. I'll finish up with the cookies and put them in the oven."

"Thanks!" said Jack. He and Annie raced to the closet and pulled on their boots. They threw on jackets, scarves, gloves, and caps.

"Be home before dark," their mom said.

"We will!" called Jack.

"Bye, Mom!" Annie shouted.

Jack and Annie slipped out of their house into the snowy cold. Their boots squeaked as they ran across their white yard and headed toward the Frog Creek woods.

At the edge of the woods, Jack stopped. He couldn't believe how beautiful the trees looked. White powder covered the branches of the hemlocks and pines.

"Look," said Annie. She pointed to two pairs of footprints that led out to the road and then back into the woods. "Somebody else has been here."

"It looks like they were walking out of the woods—but turned back," said Jack. "Let's hurry!" If the magic tree house *had* come back today, he didn't want anyone else finding it first!

Jack and Annie walked quickly through the woods, following the two sets of footprints.

"Stop!" said Annie. She pulled Jack behind a tree. "Over there!"

Through the falling snow, Jack saw two people in long, dark cloaks. They were hurrying toward a tall oak— and high in the oak was the magic tree house!

"Oh, no!" said Jack.

The tree house *was* back! And some one else had found it!

"Hey!" Jack yelled. "Stop!" The tree house had come for him and Annie—no one else!

Jack started running. Annie followed. Jack slipped and fell in the snow, but he scrambled up and kept going. By the time he and Annie got to the tree house, the two people had climbed up the rope ladder and disappeared inside.

"Come out!" Jack yelled.

"This is *our* tree house!"

神奇 树 屋

MAGIC TREE HOUSE

shouted Annie.

Two kids poked their heads out of the tree house window. They both looked like they were about thirteen years old. The boy had tousled red hair and freckles. The girl had sea-blue eyes and long, curly black hair. Their cheeks were rosy from the cold. They laughed when they saw Jack and Annie.

"Excellent!" said the boy. "We came to find you, but you have found us instead."

"Teddy!" cried Annie. "Kathleen! Hi!"

Teddy was the young sorcerer who worked with Morgan in her library in Camelot. Kathleen was the enchanted selkie girl who'd helped Jack and Annie on the summer solstice by magically turning them all into seals.

Jack was stunned. He had never imagined that their two friends from Camelot might someday visit Frog Creek! "What are you guys doing here?" he shouted.

"Climb up and we will tell you!" said Teddy.

Jack and Annie hurried up the rope ladder. When they climbed inside the tree house, Annie threw her arms around Teddy and Kathleen. "I can't believe you came to visit us!" she said.

"It pleases me to see you, Annie," said Kathleen. "And you also, Jack." Her large blue eyes sparkled.

"It pleases me, too," Jack said shyly. He still thought Kathleen was the most beautiful girl he had ever seen. Even when she'd been a seal, she'd been lovely.

"We went looking for you!" said Teddy. "We climbed down and walked through the woods to a road."

"But the road was full of monsters!" said Kathleen. "A big red creature nearly ran over us! It made a honking sound!"

"Then before we knew it, a giant black monster charged at us! It had a ferocious growl!" said Teddy. "We came back here to gather our wits."

"Those weren't monsters!" said Annie, laughing. "They were just cars!"

"Cars?" said Teddy.

"Yeah, they have motors and people drive them," said Jack.

"Motors?" said Teddy.

"It's hard to explain," said Annie. "Just remember—in our world, you have to watch out for cars every time you cross a road."

"Indeed we will," said Teddy.

"Why have you come here?" asked Jack.

"We found a message for you in Merlin's chambers," said Teddy, "and decided to deliver it ourselves."

"So we climbed into the tree house outside Morgan's library," said Kathleen. "Teddy pointed to the words *Frog Creek* in the message and made a wish to come here. The next thing we knew, we were here in these woods."

Teddy pulled a small gray stone from his cloak. "And *this* is the message we brought you," he said.

Jack took the stone from Teddy.

The message was written in tiny handwriting. Jack read it aloud:

> To Jack and Annie of Frog Creek:
> My Staff of Strength has been stolen. On the winter solstice, journey to the Land-Behind-the-Clouds. Travel toward the setting sun and retrieve my staff — or all will be lost.
>
> Merlin

"Oh, wow," said Annie. "That sounds serious."

"Yeah," said Jack. "But why didn't Merlin send us the

message himself?"

"We do not know," said Teddy. "Neither Merlin nor Morgan has been seen for days."

"Where did they go?" asked Annie.

"'Tis a mystery," said Teddy. "Last week I journeyed to the selkie cove to bring Kathleen to Camelot. She is going to be a helper in Morgan's library. But when we returned, we could not find Merlin or Morgan."

"We only found this message for you," said Kathleen.

"Aye, and I thought that when Merlin *does* return," said Teddy, "he will be greatly pleased to have his staff back. Much of his power comes from its ancient and mysterious magic."

"Wow," said Annie.

"In his message, he tells us to go to the Land-Behind-the-Clouds," said Jack. "Where's that?"

"'Tis a land far north of my cove," said Kathleen. "I have never journeyed there."

"Nor I," said Teddy. "But I have read about it in Morgan's books. 'Tis as bleak as a frozen white desert. I am eager to see it for myself."

"So you and Kathleen are coming with us?" said Annie.

"Indeed!" said Kathleen.

"Great!" said Jack and Annie together.

"If we all work together, we can do anything, aye?" said Teddy.

"Aye!" said Annie.

I hope so, thought Jack.

Annie pointed at the words *Land-Behind-the-Clouds* in Merlin's message. "Okay, ready?" she said to the others.

"Yes!" said Kathleen.

"I guess so," said Jack.

"Onward!" said Teddy.

"I wish we could all go there!" Annie said.

The tree house started to spin.

神奇 树屋
MAGIC TREE HOUSE

It spun faster and faster.

Then everything was still.

Absolutely still.

Land-Behind-the-Clouds

Jack felt the sharp bite of an icy wind. He looked out the window with the others. "Oh, man," he whispered.

The tree house was not in a tree—for there were no trees anywhere to be seen. Instead, it was sitting high on top of a steep snowdrift. Other drifts rose and fell across a vast snowy plain. Beyond the plain were hills and mountains.

"The books were right," said Teddy, his teeth chattering. "'Tis bleak here indeed."

"No, 'tis lovely," said Kathleen. "'Tis the land where the northern seal people live."

"Cool," said Annie.

Jack dug his hands into his pockets. He agreed with Teddy. The land did seem bleak—and freezing! "I wonder where Merlin's Staff of Strength is," he said, shivering.

"Let us begin our search!" said Kathleen. "The message tells us we must travel toward the setting sun."

Kathleen climbed out of the tree house window. She gathered her cloak around her and sat down on top of the snowdrift. Then she pushed off and slid down the steep slope.

"Oh, wow. Wait for me!" called Annie. She climbed out the window and followed Kathleen. Whooping, she slid to the bottom of the snowdrift. "Come on, you guys! It's fun!" she shouted.

Jack and Teddy looked at each other. "Shall we?" said Teddy. Jack nodded. He pulled his scarf tighter around his neck and followed Teddy out of the window.

Jack and Teddy sat down side by side. They pushed off and slid down the icy snowdrift. Jack couldn't help whoop-

ing, too. It *was* fun.

At the bottom of the drift, Jack and Teddy scrambled to their feet. Jack brushed the snow off his clothes. He could see his breath in the frigid air.

"It's j-just a little chilly," said Annie, hugging herself.

Only Kathleen seemed not to mind the cold. She was smiling as she lay on the ground, gazing up at the sky. *Her seal nature probably keeps her warm*, Jack thought with envy.

Teddy peered across the snowy plain. "I believe not one living creature is here but us," he said.

"Not true at all," said Kathleen. She pointed upward. "I see snow geese and whistling swans."

"I can almost see them, too," said Annie.

Kathleen stood up. She shielded her eyes and gazed across the plain. The cold sun was low in the sky. It cast long blue shadows beneath the snowdrifts. She pointed into the

distance. "And see? A white hare is leaping home before dark," she said.

Jack looked where Kathleen pointed, but he couldn't see anything moving at all.

"I see a snowy owl, too," said Kathleen, "and—oh, no!"

"What?" said Annie.

"Wolves," Kathleen said with a shudder. "They just disappeared behind a snowdrift. My people greatly fear the wolves."

"You need not be afraid. I shall protect you," said Teddy. He took Kathleen's hand. "Come! Let us make haste toward the sun!"

Together, Teddy and Kathleen headed across the snow-covered plain. Their woolen cloaks waved behind them. Annie and Jack dug their hands in their pockets and quickly followed them toward the setting sun.

As Teddy, Kathleen, Jack, and Annie trudged across the frozen plain, the sun sank closer and closer to the horizon. Its last rays poured purple-pink light over the snow.

The wind blew against Jack's face. He looked down and kept walking. The cold felt like needles on his skin. Each icy breath was painful. He hoped they found Merlin's Staff of Strength soon. He couldn't imagine anyone surviving for long in this lonely, freezing land.

Jack's thoughts were interrupted when he heard Annie calling. He looked up. The sun had completely slipped behind the horizon. In the cold twilight, the snow had faded from purple — pink to a dark shade of blue.

"Jack! Come look!" Annie called. She, Teddy, and Kathleen were standing on the slope of a huge snowdrift.

Jack hurried to join them.

"Look!" said Annie.

"Oh, man," Jack said softly.

On the other side of the snowdrift was a glimmering palace made from huge blocks of ice. Beneath the rising moon, its gleaming spires pierced the blue dusk.

"I wonder who lives there...," said Jack.

"Let us go and find out!" said Teddy.

Teddy led the way down the slope to the ice palace. Long icicles hung like spears in front of the entrance.

"It seems no one has visited this place in quite a while,"

said Kathleen.

"Indeed," said Teddy. He broke off several icicles, and they clattered to the ground. "Onward?" he said.

The others nodded.

Kicking aside the chunks of ice, Teddy led them all into the ice palace.

The Ice Wizard

The air inside the palace was even colder than the air outside. Moonlight flooded through tall arches in the walls. The floor shined like a skating rink. Thick columns of sparkling ice held up a domed ceiling.

"WELCOME, JACK AND ANNIE," boomed a voice from beyond the columns.

Jack gasped. "Is that Merlin?" he whispered.

"It does not sound like Merlin," whispered Teddy.

"But how does he know our names?" whispered Annie.

"COME, JACK AND ANNIE. I HAVE BEEN WAITING FOR YOU," bellowed the voice.

"Maybe it *is* Merlin!" said Annie. "Maybe he's just using a different voice! Come on!"

"Annie, wait!" Jack called. But

Annie had already disappeared into the sparkly room. "We have to follow her," he said to Teddy and Kathleen.

The three of them hurried after Annie. Beyond the columns, steps made of carved ice led up to a platform. Sitting on a throne on the platform was a huge bearded man.

The man on the throne was definitely *not* Merlin. He was dressed in a worn robe trimmed with dirty fur. He had a rugged, weather-beaten face, a bushy beard, and a black eye patch. He leaned forward and glared down at Annie with his one good eye.

"Who are *you*?" he demanded. "I was expecting Jack and Annie of Frog Creek."

Annie stepped toward the throne. "I am Annie and he's

Jack," she said. "And these are our friends Teddy and Kathleen. We come in peace."

"*Annie? Jack?*" the man snorted. "You are not Annie and Jack! You are far too small!"

"We're not so small," said Annie. "I'm nine. Jack's ten."

"But you are *children*," the man said with scorn. "Jack and Annie are heroes!"

"Well, I don't know if I'd call us heroes," said Annie. "But we sometimes help Merlin and Morgan le Fay."

"Annie, shhh!" said Jack. He didn't trust the man on the throne and worried that Annie was saying too much.

But Annie went on. "In fact, Merlin told us to come to the Land-Behind-the-Clouds today," she said. "He sent us a message written on a stone."

"Ah...," said the man on the throne. "Perhaps you really are Jack and Annie." He leaned forward and spoke in a low voice:

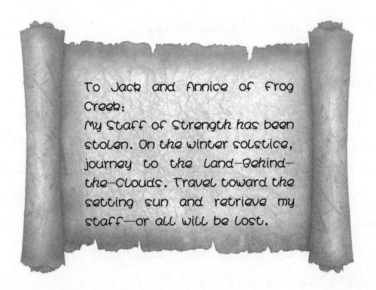

To Jack and Annice of Frog
Creek:
My Staff of Strength has been
stolen. On the winter solstice,
journey to the Land-Behind-
the-Clouds. Travel toward the
setting sun and retrieve my
staff—or all will be lost.

Jack didn't understand. "How...?"

"How do I know what was in Merlin's message?" the
man said. "I know because I wrote it myself! I hoped it would
find its way to you somehow."

Jack stepped back. So Merlin hadn't sent them on this
mission at all. The weird man on the throne had tricked them!

"Who are you?" demanded Teddy.

"I am the Ice Wizard," said the man. "The Wizard of Winter."

Teddy gulped.

Oh, no! thought Jack. They had heard about this wizard on their past Merlin missions. It was the Wizard of Winter who had put a spell on the Raven King and who had stolen the Sword of Light!

The wizard glanced coldly from Teddy to Kathleen. "And who are the two of you?"

"I am Teddy of Camelot," said Teddy. "I am an apprentice to Morgan le Fay, in training to be a sorcerer myself."

"A sorcerer?" said the wizard.

"Yes," said Teddy. "My father was a sorcerer. My mother was a wood sprite."

"And I am a selkie," said Kathleen, "one of the ancient seal people."

"So you are both from *my* world," said the Ice Wizard. "You are of no use to me." He looked back at Jack and Annie. "I am interested only in the two mortals, Jack and Annie of Frog Creek."

"Why are you interested in us?" said Jack.

"Because of what you have done for Merlin!" bellowed the Ice Wizard. "For Merlin, you found the Water of Memory and Imagination! For Merlin, you found the Diamond of Destiny! For Merlin, you found the Sword of Light! Now I want you to find something for *me*."

"What do you want us to find?" asked Annie.

The Ice Wizard grabbed the black patch covering his left eye. He yanked it off, revealing a dark, empty socket underneath.

"Yikes," Annie said softly.

"I want you to find my eye," the Ice Wizard said.

"Oh, man," said Jack. He was horrified.

"Are—are you quite serious?" said Teddy. "You want

them to find your *eye*?"

The wizard covered his empty eye socket with the patch again. "Yes," he said. "I want Jack and Annie to find my eye —and bring it back to me."

"But— why?" said Jack. "Even if we found it, we couldn't make it work. We're not medical experts or anything."

"And anyway, why can't you get your eye yourself?" said Annie. "You're a wizard!"

"DO NOT QUESTION MY ORDERS!" the wizard roared at her.

"Hey, don't yell at my sister!" said Jack.

The wizard raised a bushy eyebrow. "You are brother and sister?" he said.

"Yes," said Jack.

The wizard nodded slowly. His voice grew softer. "And you protect your sister," he said.

"We protect each other," said Jack.

"I see," whispered the wizard. Then his voice turned gruff again. "Long ago, I traded my eye for something I wanted very much. But I never got what I wanted. So now I want my eye back."

"Who did you trade with?" asked Annie.

"The Fates!" said the wizard. "I traded with the Fates! But they cheated me! And that is why I sent for you and Jack. You must go to the Fates and find my eye, and you must go alone."

"Why alone?" asked Jack.

"Because only mortals can undo a bargain with the Fates," said the Ice Wizard, "not wizards like me—nor seal girls, nor the sons of sorcerers, like your two friends."

"But Jack and I succeeded in our other missions because Teddy and Kathleen or Morgan and Merlin helped us," said Annie.

"What kind of help did they give you?" said the wizard.

"Well, mostly magic rhymes and riddles," said Annie.

"Ah. Then I shall do the same," said the wizard. He thought for a moment, then leaned forward on his throne. In a growly voice, he said:

Take my sleigh
And find your way
To the House of the Norns
In the curve of the bay.
Pay them whatever
They tell you to pay.
And bring back my eye
By break of day.

The wizard reached into the folds of his ragged robe and pulled out a thick string with a row of knots. "This wind-string will speed you on your journey," he said. He tossed the string to Jack.

What's a wind-string? Jack wondered. *And who are the Norns?*

Before Jack could ask any questions, the Ice Wizard pointed at him. "Now listen carefully to this warning," he said. "Beware the white wolves of the night. They may follow you on your quest. Never let them catch up with you. If they catch you, they will eat you!"

Jack felt a chill run down his spine.

The Ice Wizard picked up a carved wooden stick from the floor beside his throne. Its smooth, polished wood glowed in the moonlight.

Teddy gasped. "'Tis merlin's Staff of Strength!" he said.

"Indeed," said the wizard. He turned to Jack and Annie. "Go now and find my eye," he said. "Or you will never see Merlin and Morgan le Fay again."

"What have you done with them?" cried Annie.

神奇 树屋

MAGIC TREE HOUSE

The wizard stared at her coldly. "I will not tell you," he said. "You will see them again *only* if you return my eye before the break of day."

"But—" said Annie.

"No more questions!" said the wizard. "Be on your way!" Before any of them could speak, the Ice Wizard slashed the air with Merlin's Staff of Strength and shouted a spell—"OW-NIGH!"

A flash of blue fire shot from the end of the staff. In an instant, Jack, Annie, Teddy, and Kathleen found themselves outside the palace in the freezing night.

Take My Sleigh

Jack sat on the frozen ground. Annie, Teddy, and Kathleen sat nearby. They were all too shocked to speak. The night was quiet. Overhead the full moon shined brightly, and a few cold stars twinkled in the clear sky.

Finally Annie broke the silence. "I wonder what he did to Merlin and Morgan," she said.

"I wonder where you will find his eye," said Teddy.

"I wonder how we'll carry it around," said Jack.

"And I wonder if the wolves are near," said Kathleen. She stood up and looked around, pulling her cloak tightly around her.

"Well, does anyone remember the Ice Wizard's rhyme?" said Teddy.

"Yes," said Kathleen. She repeated the rhyme perfetly by heart:

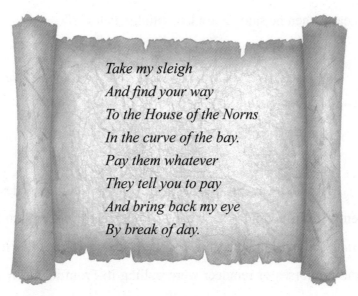

Take my sleigh
And find your way
To the House of the Norns
In the curve of the bay.
Pay them whatever
They tell you to pay
And bring back my eye
By break of day.

"What are *Norns*?" asked Jack.

"I have read about the Norns in Morgan's books," said Teddy. "They are known as the Sisters of Fate. They spend their days weaving great tapestries. Their weaving deter mines the fate of all who live in the Land-Behind-the-Clouds."

"So the Norns have his eye?" said Jack. "That's who he

meant when he said he 'traded with the Fates'?"

"It would seem so," said Teddy.

"He said we should take his sleigh to find them," said Annie. "Where's his sleigh?"

"Look," said Kathleen, pointing. "'Tis there."

"Oh, wow," said Annie.

Not far away, a strange-looking silver sleigh glided silently from behind a snowbank. The sleigh looked like a small sailing ship with shiny runners. No one was steering it, and no horses or reindeer were pulling it. From its mast, a white sail drooped in the still air.

As the sleigh slid to a stop, an eerie howl shattered the calm of the windless night.

"Wolves!" cried Teddy. "Let us make haste!"

Kathleen grabbed his arm. "Do not run," she said. "If we run, they will chase us."

"Yes, of course," said Teddy. "They must not see that

we are afraid."

Another howl shattered the air.

"Run!" cried Teddy.

They all charged across the snow to the sleigh and scrambled into it. Jack and Kathleen stood at the front, and Annie and Teddy stood at the back.

"There they are!" cried Teddy, pointing. "The white wolves of the night!"

Jack turned and saw two large white wolves dashing across the plain in the moonlight. As the wolves ran toward the sleigh, their big paws scattered snow around them.

"Go, go, go!" Jack cried, clutching the front of the sleigh.

But the sleigh didn't move. And the wolves kept coming. "How can we make it go?" cried Jack.

"Use the wind-string!" said Teddy.

Jack pulled the knotted string the wizard had given him

out of his pocket. "Use it *how*?" he shouted.

"Untie a knot!" said Teddy.

Jack pulled off his gloves. His fingers were trembling as he tried to untie one of the knots. *This is crazy!* he thought. *How can untying a knot in a string help us?* But soon he managed to loosen one of the knots.

A cold breeze began blowing from behind the sleigh. It ruffled the sail overhead.

"Untie another!" shouted Teddy. "Hurry!"

Jack quickly untied a second knot. The breeze grew stronger, and the sail filled out a bit more. The sleigh's shiny runners began sliding across the snow.

"Yay!" called Annie. "It works!"

"Yes, but not nearly swiftly enough!" said Teddy.

Jack looked back. The two white wolves had almost caught up with them. They were yelping and running behind the sleigh. Their mouths were open, showing their sharp teeth.

Jack quickly untied a third knot. A cold wind blasted the sail. It opened with a snap, and the sleigh shot forward!

"Stand fast!" cried Teddy.

Jack, Annie, and Kathleen held tightly to the sides of the sleigh to keep from falling out. Teddy grabbed the rudder and steered them over the snow, away from the ice palace.

The wizard's sleigh zoomed across the frozen ground, leaving the white wolves in its wake. Their yelping noises grew fainter and fainter, until they could be heard no more.

The wind kept pushing the silver sleigh over the ice and snow. The runners made *swish-swish* sounds as they slid over the moonlit plain. The square sail billowed in the wind, like the sail of a Viking ship. With the wolves far behind, the ride was really fun, but cold.

"How did you know untying knots would make the wind blow?" Jack asked Teddy.

"'Tis an ancient magic," said Teddy. "I have read of

wind-strings but had never seen one."

"It's a good thing you read so much," said Annie.

"Oh, look!" said Kathleen. "Hares and foxes!"

"Where?" said Annie.

"There!" Kathleen pointed into the dark distance. "Playing in the snow! And listen! Whistling swans—overhead, behind that cloud."

"Wow," said Annie.

Jack was amazed by Kathleen's power to see and hear so many things. As before, the moonlit landscape seemed completely empty to him.

"Where are you steering us?" Annie asked Teddy.

"I have no idea!" said Teddy, laughing.

"We're supposed to go to a curve of a bay to find the Norns," said Annie.

"Then turn left and follow the swans!" said Kathleen, pointing across the snowy plain. "They are flying toward the

sea!"

Teddy swerved the sleigh to the left. For a while, they bounced up and down over the snow. Then the ride grew smoother.

"We are on sea ice now!" said Kathleen. "Seals are beneath! I see their breathing holes! Perhaps we should stop."

"Indeed!" said Teddy as they whizzed along. "But how?"

"Try *tying* a knot!" said Annie.

"Excellent idea!" said Teddy. "Jack?"

Jack yanked off his gloves. With cold, shaky fingers, he tied a knot in the string. The wind lessened a bit. The sleigh began to slow down. He tied another. The sail started to droop.

"Hooray!" said Annie.

Jack tied a third knot and the wind completely died away. The sleigh glided to a stop.

"Well done!" said Teddy.

"Thanks," said Jack. He tucked the string back in his pocket and looked around. "I wonder if this is where the Norns live."

"I will ask," said Kathleen.

Ask *who?* thought Jack.

Kathleen climbed out of the sleigh. She walked over the sea ice, studying it closely. Then she stopped above a small hole.

Kathleen knelt down and spoke softly in selkie language. Then she put her ear close to the hole in the ice and listened.

A moment later, she stood up. "The seal told me the curve of the bay lies just beyond those sea rocks," she said, pointing. "That is where we will find the Norns."

"Great," said Annie.

Jack, Annie, Teddy, and Kathleen crunched over the frozen sea under the bright moon. They walked through a

narrow passage between the sea rocks. When they stepped out from the passage, they stopped.

"There 'tis," said Teddy.

About fifty yards away was a large, snowy white mound. Smoke was coming from a chimney on top of the mound. Lantern light flickered from a small, round window.

"I know you must bargain for the Ice Wizard's eye alone," said Teddy. "But I would at least like to take a peek at the Norns."

He moved quietly to the window and peered into the house. The others joined him. They saw a large fire burning on a hearth. In its rosy glow, three strange creatures were weaving at a big loom. Jack caught his breath. Their appearance was shocking.

The three Sisters of Fate were as skinny as skeletons. They all had straggly hair, long noses, and huge, bulging eyes. Their crooked, bony fingers fluttered over a large

tapestry. Around the room other tapestries were stacked to the ceiling.

"They look like witches in a fairy tale," whispered Annie.

"Aye, but they are not witches," said Teddy. "Every cloth they weave is the history of a life."

"Wow," said Annie.

"Well, good luck," said Teddy. "Kathleen and I will wait out here while you go inside and ask for the wizard's eye."

Suddenly a terrible howl pierced the silence.

"Yikes!" said Annie.

"The wolves!" said Kathleen.

Teddy hurried to the door and threw it open. "Everyone inside!" he said.

And all four of them scrambled into the House of the Norns.

The Norns

Teddy slammed the door against the wolves. Jack caught his breath.

"Welcome!" the three Norns said in unison. They all looked exactly alike, except they wore gowns of different colors—blue, brown, and gray.

"How are you, Jack, Annie, Teddy, and Kathleen?" said the blue Norn.

"We're good *now*," said Annie.

Jack was amazed that the Norns knew all their names. Despite their strange appearance, their friendly smiles and twinkling eyes put him at ease. In their cozy house, he began to feel warm for the first time since they had left home.

"Was your journey pleasant?" asked the brown Norn.

"Yes. We came in the Ice Wizard's sleigh," said Annie.

"With the help of a wind-string," said Teddy. Jack held up the string to show them.

The gray Norn cackled. "Yes, we know! I like a string

with knots," she said.

"A string without knots would be a boring string indeed!" said the blue Norn.

"A *life* without knots would be a boring life indeed!" chimed in the brown Norn.

As they spoke, the Norns kept weaving. Their bulging eyes never blinked. Jack sensed that they never closed their eyes—or stopped their work.

"Sorry to bother you," said Annie. "But Jack and I need the eye of the Ice Wizard of Winter so we can save our friends Merlin and Morgan."

"We know," said the blue Norn. "We are weaving the story of the Ice Wizard now. Come look."

Jack moved with the others to the loom. Dozens of tiny pictures were woven into the tapestry. The threads were all wintry colors— blues, grays, and browns.

"The pictures tell the story of the wizard's life,"

explained the brown Norn.

One picture showed two children playing together. Another showed a boy running after a swan. Another showed two white wolves—and another showed an eye in a circle.

"What's the story of the eye?" Jack asked.

"Long ago, the Ice Wizard came to us seeking all the wisdom of the world," said the gray Norn. "We said we would give him wisdom if he gave us one of his eyes. He agreed to the bargain."

"The wizard doesn't seem very wise," said Annie.

"Indeed he is not," said the brown Norn. "We planted the seeds of wisdom in his heart, but they never grew."

"Why did you want his eye?" asked Jack.

"We wished to give it to the Frost Giant," said the blue Norn.

"*The Frost Giant?*" said Teddy. "Who is the Frost Giant?"

"He is neither magician nor mortal," said the blue Norn. "He is a blind force of nature that spares nothing in his path."

"We hoped the Frost Giant would use the wizard's eye to *see* the beauty of the world, so he might choose to *care* for it rather than destroy it," said the brown Norn. "But alas, the Frost Giant does not use our gift at all! Instead, he keeps it hidden away—right where we left it!"

"Where's that?" asked Annie.

"The Frost Giant sleeps inside the Hollow Hill," said the gray Norn.

"In the Hollow Hill is a hole," said the blue Norn.

"In the hole is a hailstone," said the brown Norn.

"And in the heart of the hailstone hides the wizard's eye," said the gray Norn.

Jack closed his eyes and repeated:

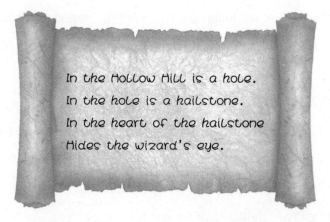

In the Hollow Hill is a hole.
In the hole is a hailstone.
In the heart of the hailstone
Hides the wizard's eye.

"Yes!" said the gray Norn. "That is where you must go. But beware: *You must never look directly at the Frost Giant. Anyone who looks directly at the Frost Giant will freeze to death at once.*"

Jack shivered and nodded.

"Well, we'd better get going," said Annie. "Thanks for your help. The Ice Wizard's rhyme tells us to pay you whatever you ask us to pay."

The Norns looked at each other. "I like that weaving around her neck," the gray Norn said to her sisters. "'Tis

red like the fiery dawn." The other two Norns nodded eagerly.

"My scarf? " said Annie. "Sure. Here." She took off her red woolen scarf and placed it on the floor near the Norns' loom.

"Lovely!" said the blue Norn. "Perhaps we will stop weaving fates and start weaving scarves!"

The other Norns cackled. "Well, go now, " said the gray Norn. "Travel toward the North Star. When you reach the snowy hills, look for the one whose peak is missing."

Jack, Annie, and Teddy started toward the door, but Kathleen stayed behind. "Forgive me, but I have one more question, " she said. She pointed to the picture of the swan and the boy on the tapestry. "What is this story?"

"'Tis a sad tale," said the gray Norn. "The Ice Wizard had a younger sister who loved him more than anything in the world. One day they fought over something foolish. He lost his temper and told her to leave him alone forever. She ran down to the sea in tears. There she found a flock of swan maidens. They gave her a white feathered dress. She put on the dress and became a swan maiden herself. She flew away with the others and never returned."

"After that the Ice Wizard was never the same," said the blue Norn. "When his sister left, he grew cold and mean-spirited. 'Twas as if his sister took his heart with her when she flew away."

"That *is* sad," said Annie. "How will the Ice Wizard's story end?"

"You—not we—will determine the threads we weave next," said the brown Norn.

"We will?" said Annie.

"Yes," said the gray Norn. "Our powers are fading. Our plans no longer work the way we expect them to. The Ice Wizard has no wisdom! The Frost Giant has no sight! *You* must go now and finish the story."

The three sisters smiled at their visitors. Their skinny fingers fluttered over their weaving like butterflies over flowers.

Jack couldn't help smiling back at them. But then he thought about Merlin and Morgan. He thought about all the dangers waiting outside. "One last question," he said. "What's the story of the two white wolves?"

"Oh, the wolves!" said the blue Norn. "Do not fear the wolves! A life without wolves would be a boring life indeed!" Her two sisters smiled in agreement. For the moment, their smiles made Jack feel unafraid of the white wolves—and the Ice Wizard and the Frost Giant, too.

"Good-bye! Good-bye! Good-bye!" said the three

sisters.

Jack and the others waved good-bye. Then they slipped out of the House of the Norns and into the icy night.

In the Hollow Hill

Standing in the cold, Jack felt afraid again. There were big paw prints in the moonlit snow all around the house.

"The wolves were here," said Kathleen.

"Perhaps we should go back inside," said Teddy.

"No," said Kathleen. "We must walk with Jack and Annie back to the sleigh and send them on their journey to the Hollow Hill."

"Yes, of course," said Teddy, nodding.

As they all headed cautiously toward the rocks, Jack glanced back at the House of the Norns. He wished they could return to its cozy warmth.

Kathleen put her hand on his shoulder. "Come," she said. "You must hurry."

Jack trudged with the others through the passage in the rocks. When they got to the other side, there was no sign of the two white wolves. The silver sleigh was waiting in the moonlight. Jack and Annie climbed inside it.

"Can't you come with us?"Jack asked Teddy and Kathleen. "Remember you said if we all work together, we can do anything?"

"Aye," said Teddy. "But what the Ice Wizard said is true. Only mortals can undo a bargain with the Fates."

"Do not fear," said Kathleen. "We will be with you in spirit. And we will meet you back at the wizard's palace at dawn."

"How will you get there?" asked Annie.

"I have a few rhymes I can try," said Teddy, smiling.

"And I have a bit of selkie magic," said Kathleen.

"And we have our wind-string!" said Annie.

"Hasten, then, to the Hollow Hill," said Kathleen.

"And remember what the Norns told you," said Teddy. "*Never* look at the Frost Giant."

"I know," said Jack. He pulled out the wind-string. He took off his gloves and untied a knot. A breeze began to blow.

Jack untied a second knot. The breeze grew stronger, the sail unfurled, and the runners slid forward.

Jack untied a third knot. The wind blew hard. The white sail snapped, and the sleigh took off through the night.

"Stand fast!" Teddy called after them.

Jack and Annie waved good-bye to Teddy and Kathleen as the sleigh slid swiftly over the sea ice. Soon the sleigh bumped onto the snow-covered plain and veered off sharply to the right.

"No, toward the North Star!" Jack called to Annie.

Annie turned the rudder, steering the sleigh back on course. They sailed toward the bright star in the distance.

As the silver runners swished across the windswept snow, Jack braced himself against the cold. He kept a lookout for the white wolves, but he didn't see any sign of them as the sleigh sped across the moonlit plain.

Soon he could see a row of snow-covered hills in the

distance. "Look!" he said. "There it is!" He pointed to one of the hills—the only one without a peak.

"Tie her down!" Annie shouted.

Jack tied a knot in the string, and the sleigh began to slow down. He tied a second, then a third. The wind died down completely, and the sleigh coasted to a stop at the foot of the Hollow Hill. Jack and Annie climbed out.

Jack looked up at the steep white slope. "How do we get inside?" he said.

"I don't know," said Annie. "How do you think the Frost Giant gets inside?"

"Oh...the Frost Giant," said Jack. He really wished Teddy and Kathleen were with them. He felt as if part of their team was missing.

Annie seemed to read his thoughts. "We can do it," she said. "We have to—for Morgan and Merlin."

Jack nodded. "You're right," he said. They studied the

hill in the moonlight.

"Up there—is that an opening?" said Annie.

"Maybe," said Jack. "Let's climb up and check it out." When they climbed a little way up the hill, Jack could clearly see a break in the snow-covered slope.

"Let's see if it leads inside!" said Annie.

"Wait, what about the Frost Giant?" said Jack.

"I have a feeling he's not here right now," said Annie. "We'd better go in and find the wizard's eye before he comes back."

"Okay," said Jack. "But be careful!"

They scurried farther up the slope. When they came to the opening, they stepped through the huge crack into the hill.

Jack and Annie found themselves on a ledge above a deep, rounded hollow. Moonlight flooded down through the open hilltop. At the bottom of the hollow was a flat spot where

it looked as if the snow had been blown in circles.

"That must be where the giant sleeps!" said Annie.

"Yeah, and it's probably where he hides the eye," said Jack. "We just have to find a hole. Remember?" He repeated what the Norns had said:

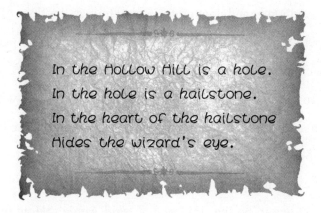

In the Hollow Hill is a hole.
In the hole is a hailstone.
In the heart of the hailstone
Hides the wizard's eye.

"Right," said Annie.

Jack looked down at the snowy swirl. He looked back at Annie. "Onward?"

"Onward," she whispered.

Jack and Annie scrambled down into the hollow.

Stepping carefully through the silver moonlight, they studied the ground, looking for the hole.

Annie stumbled and fell. "Whoa!" she said. "I think I just found the hole! I stepped in it!"

"Really?" said Jack. He knelt down beside her.

Annie reached down into a small hole in the floor of the hollow. "There's something in here!" she said. She pulled out a chunk of ice the size of an egg. "The hailstone!"

In the dim light, it was impossible to see if anything was inside the ice chunk. "We don't know if this is the right hailstone," said Jack. "We'll have to wait till daylight to see if the eye's in there."

"It has to be the right one," said Annie. "How many hailstones are hidden in a hole in a hollow hill?"

"Good point," said Jack.

Annie turned the hailstone over in her hand. "Maybe the eye is looking at us now," she said.

"That's scientifically impossible," said Jack. "An eye can't see unless it's connected to a brain."

"Yeah, and a string can't make the wind blow, either," said Annie. "Forget science in this place. Wait—" She caught her breath. "Did you feel that?"

"Feel what?" said Jack.

"The ground's shaking," said Annie.

Jack *did* feel the ground trembling. He heard a strange sound, too—a loud huffing sound coming from outside the hill—*HUFFFF, HUFFFF, HUFFFF...* It sounded like breathing!

"The giant's back!" said Annie.

"Oh, no!" cried Jack.

The ground kept rumbling. The breathing sounds got louder.

"Hide the hailstone!" said Jack.

Annie shoved the ice chunk into her pocket.

HUFFFF, HUFFFF, HUFFFF... It sounded like the giant was entering the hollow!

"He's coming!" said Annie.

"Hide!" whispered Jack.

Jack pulled Annie into the shadows. He remembered the gray Norn's warning: *Anyone who looks directly at the Frost Giant will freeze to death at once.*

"Whatever you do, *don't look at him!*" he whispered to Annie.

Crouching in the dark, they buried their faces in their hands and waited...

7

The Frost Giant

HUFFFF，*HUFFFF*，*HUFFFFF*... With each breath from the Frost Giant，a blast of cold wind swept through the hollow.

Jack trembled. He felt chilled to the bone. *HUFFFF*，*HUFFFF*，*HUFFFFF*...

The giant's breathing grew louder and stronger. Jack squeezed his eyes shut as icy，wet wind rushed against his body.

HUFFFF，*HUFFFF*，*HUFFFFF*...

Jack crouched lower and held on tightly to Annie.

HUFFFF，*HUFFFF*，*HUFFFFF*...

The giant's breath howled like a hundred ghosts through the hollow. Jack thought of the blue Norn's words：*He is a blind force of nature that spares nothing in his path...*

But then the giant's breathing seemed to grow a bit softer. *What's happening?* Jack wondered.

The breathing grew softer and softer. "Maybe he's go-

ing to sleep," Annie whispered.

The breathing became calm and steady. The wind died to a light breeze.

"I think the Frost Giant is sleeping," Annie whispered. "We should try to sneak out of here."

"Okay, but keep your eyes down. Just look at the ground!" whispered Jack.

"Right," whispered Annie.

Their heads bowed, Jack and Annie crept cautiously across the floor of the hollow and began climbing up toward the crack. Jack's teeth chattered, but he couldn't tell if it was from cold or fear.

Suddenly a deafening roar shook the night! The Frost Giant screamed with windy rage! He was awake!

Jack was blown to the ground. He tried to crawl across the snow, but he didn't know which way to go, and he was afraid to look up.

"Jack! This way!" Annie's voice called above the roar of the giant's breath. She helped him up and they struggled together against the wind. Finally they came to the crack in the wall.

Jack and Annie scrambled through the crack. Outside, the wild wind knocked them over, and they tumbled down the side of the hill.

The wind swirled the snow across the plain. "Annie! Annie!" Jack called. Where was she? Where was the sleigh? He couldn't see anything. He couldn't stay on his feet.

The wind roared even louder. An avalanche of snow came crashing down the hillside. When it hit the ground, the snow exploded into great clouds of white powder.

"Jack! Jack!"

Jack heard Annie's voice in the screaming wind. He tried to stand up. But snow kept falling on top of him, until he was completely covered.

As Jack lay buried under the snow，all his strength left his body. He knew he should dig his way out，but he was too cold and too tired. He was too tired to look for Annie. He was too tired to fight the Frost Giant. Instead，he closed his eyes and drifted into an icy sleep.

*　　*　　*

Jack dreamed that cold fur was brushing against his face. He dreamed that a wolf was digging around him，nudging him，pushing him，sniffing him...

Jack opened his eyes. He felt dazed. At first he couldn't see. But he could feel that he wasn't buried in snow anymore. He wiped off his glasses. He saw a low moon and some stars in a clear sky.

The Frost Giant must have left，Jack thought. But then he heard a panting noise. He sat up and looked around. One of the white wolves was crouching right behind him!

Jack scrambled to his feet. "Go away!" he shouted.

The wolf stepped back and growled.

"Go! Go! Go!" shouted Jack. He picked up handfuls of snow and threw them at the wolf.

The wolf backed away a few more feet. Jack looked around wildly. Annie was lying very still on top of the snow. The other white wolf was sniffing and pawing at her.

Jack's anger made him fearless. "Leave her alone!" he shouted. "Go away!" He scooped up more snow and threw it.

The wolf stepped back.

"GO! GO!"shouted Jack."Get away! Leave us alone!" He glared angrily at the two white wolves.

The wolves stared back at Jack. Their yellow eyes gleamed.

"I'm not kidding—GO!" shouted Jack.

Jack stared fiercely at the wolves. Finally the wolves looked away. They glanced at each other and then slowly backed off. They looked at Jack and Annie one last time.

神奇 树 屋
MAGIC TREE HOUSE

Then they turned and trotted away over the snow.

Jack rushed to Annie. He knelt beside her and lifted her head. "Wake up! Wake up!" he said.

Annie opened her eyes.

"You okay?" Jack asked.

"Yes... I dreamed about white wolves," Annie murmured.

"Me too!" said Jack. "And then when I woke up, they were here! They were about to eat us!"

"Really?" Annie sat up and looked around.

"Yeah, but I scared them off," said Jack.

"What about the Frost Giant?" Annie said.

"He's gone, too," said Jack. "Come on. Let's get out of here!" Jack helped Annie up from the snow. "Do you still have the wizard's eye?"

Annie felt in her pocket. "Got it," she said.

"Good." Jack looked around. Beyond the heaps of

fallen snow, the silver sleigh was waiting for them. Overhead, the sky had turned to a light shade of gray.

"It's almost dawn," said Jack. "Remember what the wizard said? We have to bring back his eye by the break of day—or we'll never see Merlin or Morgan again!"

Jack held Annie's hand and they trudged together through the snow. When they got to the sleigh, they climbed inside. Annie took her place at the rudder. Jack pulled out the wind-string and untied a knot.

The breeze rocked the sleigh. Jack untied a second knot, and the sail began to fill. He untied a third, and the silver sleigh moved forward, gliding over the white ground.

Swish—swish—swish. The sleigh moved through the thick snow and away from the Hollow Hill. As they sailed over the white plain, the sky was turning from gray to pale pink.

"We have to go faster!" said Annie.

Jack untied a fourth knot. The wind whistled in his ears. The sleigh picked up speed. Annie steered it past the rocks and over the sea ice. She steered it over the plain, south to the palace of the Ice Wizard.

When the sleigh drew close to the palace, Jack tied a knot, and they began to slow down. He tied three more, and the sleigh came to a stop.

Jack and Annie looked around in the faint, cold light. "I wonder where Teddy and Kathleen are," said Annie. "They said they'd meet us here at dawn."

Jack studied the vast white plain, but he saw no sign of their friends. He wished he had Kathleen's vision. "I hope they're okay," he said. "I hope they didn't run into the white wolves."

"I have a feeling the wolves wouldn't hurt them," said Annie. "The wolf in my dream seemed nice."

"Dream wolves are different from real wolves," said

Jack.

"I don't think we can wait for them," said Annie. "The eye has to be back by the time the sun comes up."

"The eye!" said Jack. "We never looked to see if it was inside the hailstone."

Annie reached in her pocket and pulled out the hailstone. She held it up.

Jack gasped. Staring out at him from inside the ice was an eyeball. It was about the size of a large marble. The eyeball was white with a sparkling blue center.

"Oh, man," whispered Jack.

"It's beautiful, isn't it?" said Annie.

"I don't know about that." Jack felt a little queasy. Seeing an eye outside of a human head was too weird for him. "Put it away for now," he said.

Annie put the hailstone back in her pocket. Jack looked around again. The sky had brightened from pale pink to red.

A thin sliver of the sun was peeking over the horizon.

"The sun!" cried Jack. "Hurry!" He and Annie jumped out of the sleigh and charged toward the palace.

When they got to the entrance, Annie stopped. "Look!" she said, pointing to big paw prints in the snow. "Wolf tracks!"

"Oh, no," said Jack. "Do you think the white wolves are inside? That's weird."

"It doesn't matter! We have to go in! Hurry!" said Annie. They rushed into the palace—just as the fiery ball of the sun rose over the horizon.

Return of the Eye

神奇 树 屋
MAGIC TREE HOUSE

Jack and Annie walked through the front hall of the palace, past the ice columns, and into the wizard's throne room. The walls and floor glittered with the brilliant, cold light of dawn.

"Un-oh," said Jack.

The wizard was waiting for them—and the two white wolves were sleeping on either side of his throne. Jack was confused. *Why are they here?* he wondered. *Do they belong to the wizard?*

The wolves lifted their heads and sniffed the air. Their ears pricked up. When they caught sight of Jack and Annie, they sprang to their feet. They stared at them with piercing yellow eyes.

The Ice Wizard was staring intently at Jack and Annie, too. "Well?" he said. "Did you bring back my eye?"

"Yes," said Jack.

Annie took the hailstone out of her pocket and held it up

to the wizard. Jack watched the wolves nervously as the hailstone passed from Annie's small hand into the wizard's large, rough hand.

The wizard stared down at the chunk of ice. Then he looked at Jack and Annie. "Indeed, you *are* heroes," he said breathlessly.

"Not really," Jack murmured.

The wizard looked again at his eye inside the hailstone. Then, with a quick movement, he slammed the ice chunk against the arm of his throne.

Jack and Annie gasped and stepped back. The wizard slammed the hailstone against his throne again. This time, the ice cracked.

The wizard gently pried his eye out of the heart of the hailstone. He lifted the frozen eyeball into the air and studied it in the light. Then, with an eager cry, he ripped off his eye patch.

Jack and Annie watched in amazement as the wizard fitted the eye into its dark, empty socket. Jack held his breath. He was horrified, yet fascinated. He couldn't imagine someone just shoving an eye back into his head.

The wizard slowly lowered his hand. He seemed to be holding his breath. He had two eyes. But the new one didn't move. It looked as if it was still frozen.

Jack grew worried. If the eye didn't work, the wizard might not help them. "We—we brought you your eye," he said. "So can you tell us where Merlin and Morgan are now?"

The wizard jerked his head to look at Jack. He covered one eye with his hand. Then he covered the other. In a frenzy, he went back and forth, covering and uncovering each eye.

Finally the wizard dropped his hand and roared, "NO!" The wizard's howl shook the ice columns. "You have tricked me!"

"No we haven't," said Annie.

"This eye is useless!" cried the wizard. "It has no life! No sight!"

"But that's the eye you gave to the Norns," said Annie. "You promised if we brought it back, you'd give us Merlin and Morgan."

The two white wolves threw back their heads and howled.

"NO!" cried the wizard. "You tricked me! You tricked me!"

"Let's get out of here," whispered Jack. He pulled Annie toward the ice columns.

"STOP!" shouted

the wizard. "YOU CANNOT ESCAPE ME!" He grabbed Merlin's Staff of Strength. The wolves growled and yelped. The wizard pointed the staff at Jack and Annie. He started to say a spell—"RO-EEE—"

"WAIT!" someone yelled. Teddy burst into the throne room. "Wait! Wait!"

The wizard held his staff in the air. He stared wildly at Teddy. His face was twisted with rage.

"We have something for you!" Teddy shouted at the wizard. "Kathleen!" he called.

Kathleen stepped out from behind the ice columns. With her was a young woman with long braids. The woman wore a flowing dress. Around her shoulders was a white feathered cloak. Her eyes rested on the wizard, and a radiant smile spread over her face. She began walking slowly toward the throne.

The wizard lowered Merlin's Staff of Strength. He stared

back at the young woman. All the color drained from his face. For a long moment, he was as still as a statue. Then an ice-blue tear leaked out of his frozen eye and ran down his white cheek.

Jack and Annie stood with Kathleen and Teddy. They all watched the young woman and the Ice Wizard gaze silently at each other.

"Is she his sister, the swan maiden?" whispered Annie.

"Yes," whispered Kathleen.

The swan maiden spoke to the Ice Wizard in a strange language—"*Val-ee-ven-o-wan.*"

The wizard did not answer. Tears flowed gently now from both his eyes.

"*Val-ee-ven-o-wan,*" the swan maiden said again.

"What's she saying?" Jack asked.

"She is saying, *I have come back to forgive you,*" said Kathleen.

The wizard stood up. He walked down the steps from

his throne. He gently touched the swan maiden's face, as if to make sure she was real. Then he answered her softly in the strange language. *"Fel-o-wan."*

"How did you find her?" Jack asked Teddy.

"A seal took us under the ice to the Isle of the Swans," said Teddy.

"When we found her, I told her how much the wizard has missed her," said Kathleen. "I also told her about the two of you and how you always help each other. I told her she should return to her brother and be his friend again."

The wizard and his sister kept speaking softly to each other in their strange language. Warm sunlight shimmered through the palace windows.

Annie stepped forward. "Um—excuse me," she said.

The wizard looked at her. "My sister has returned home," he said with wonder. "I can see with both eyes now. I can see perfectly."

"I'm glad," said Annie. "But now you must give Merlin and Morgan back to us."

The wizard looked at his sister. She nodded. The wizard held out Merlin's Staff of Strength. "Use this to bring them back," he said. "Hold it tightly and call out for them." He gave the staff to Annie.

Annie could barely lift it by herself. "Hold it with me, Jack," she said.

Jack stepped forward and grabbed the magic staff. The smooth, golden wood felt warm and vibrant in his hands.

As they gripped the staff together, Annie threw back her head and called out: "Merlin and Morgan, come back!"

A long burst of blue light shot out of the end of the staff —and flashed toward the two white wolves.

Suddenly wolf eyes changed into human eyes! Wolf noses changed into human noses! Wolf mouths changed into human mouths! Wolf ears into human ears! Wolf paws into

human hands and feet! Wolf fur into long red cloaks!

The two white wolves were gone，and a man and a woman stood in their places.

Wisdom of the Heart

"Merlin! Morgan!" shouted Annie.

Teddy and Kathleen cried out in amazement.

Annie rushed to Morgan and hugged her.

Jack was filled with giddy relief. "Hi!" he said. "Hi!"

"Welcome back, sir!" Teddy said to Merlin.

"Thank you," said Merlin. He looked at Jack and Annie. "And thank you for turning us back into ourselves."

"We didn't know you and Morgan were the wolves!" Annie said.

"We were following you so we could help you," said Morgan.

"The wizard told us that if you caught up with us, you would eat us!" said Jack.

"Really?" said Morgan.

They all looked at the Ice Wizard. Standing with his sister, he stared guiltily at Morgan and Merlin.

"I feared that if they got close to you, they might dis-

cover who you were," he said. "But I will do no more harm,
I promise—for I can see clearly now." The wizard looked
back at his sister, and his blue eyes shined with joy.

"You can see because you have your heart back," said
Morgan. "It was not only your eye that was missing—it was
also your heart. We see with our hearts as well as our eyes."

"And now perhaps you can find the wisdom you were
seeking from the Norns," said Merlin, "for wisdom is knowl-
edge learned with the heart as well as the head."

The Ice Wizard nodded. "Please find it in *your* hearts to
forgive me," he said. "Use my sleigh to take you safely home."

"Yes, indeed, we must leave now," said Morgan. "We
have been gone from Camelot too long."

"The next time you come to Camelot, my friend, you
must come as a guest," said Merlin, "not as a thief in the
night."

"And you must bring your sister also," Morgan said to

the wizard.

"Indeed I will," the wizard said.

Merlin looked at Jack, Annie, Teddy, and Kathleen. "Is everyone ready to leave now?" he asked.

"Yes, sir," they all answered together.

Merlin looked at the Staff of Strength in Jack's hands.

"Oh! Sorry, I almost forgot," said Jack. He handed the heavy staff to Merlin.

As soon as Merlin held the Staff of Strength, he seemed more powerful. "Let us be off!" he said briskly.

Merlin and Morgan led the way out of the throne room, their red cloaks billowing behind them. Teddy and Kathleen followed, and Jack and Annie hurried after them.

Just before they left the room, Jack and Annie glanced back at the Ice Wizard and his swan sister. They were deep in conversation again.

"They haven't seen each other for years," said Annie.

"They must have a lot to talk about."

"Yeah," said Jack. He couldn't imagine not seeing Annie for years. "Come on, let's go." He took her hand and pulled her out of the throne room, through the front hall, and into the cold dawn.

Jack and Annie followed their four Camelot friends to the wizard's sleigh. Everyone climbed in.

Annie sat at the rudder. Jack stood at the front. He pulled out the wind-string and untied a knot. The sleigh rocked forward. He untied another, and the sleigh started moving very slowly.

The sleigh was heavier than before, so Jack quickly untied two more knots. The sleigh bolted across the snow.

"Stand fast!" said Teddy.

As the sleigh swished through the dawn, Annie turned to Morgan and Merlin. "I have a question," she said. "Can you tell us what the giant looks like—the Frost Giant?"

Merlin smiled. "There is no Frost Giant," he said.

"*What?*" said Kathleen and Teddy.

"Sure there is," said Annie. "We heard his breathing!"

"He nearly froze us to death!" said Jack.

"At night, the wind often swirls through the Hollow Hill like a cyclone," said Merlin. "You experienced one of those storms."

"But what about the Norns' story of giving the wizard's eye to the Frost Giant as a gift?" said Jack.

"Many ancient peoples believe that the forces of nature are actual giants or monsters," said Morgan. "The Norns are the last of their kind. They hold to the idea that the Frost Giant is a living creature who haunts the Hollow Hill. In truth, the Frost Giant never accepted their gift because there is no Frost Giant."

Jack shook his head. "We believed what the Norns believed. They told us we'd freeze to death if we looked

directly at the Frost Giant."

"And we believed what the wizard told us, too," said Annie, "that the wolves would eat us if they caught up to us!"

"People often try to convince us that the world is scarier than it truly is," said Morgan.

Right now the world didn't seem at all scary to Jack. Everything was calm and bright. Soft, rose-colored light was breaking through the morning clouds.

"Today is the first day after the winter solstice," said Morgan. "Today the light starts to return. The days will grow longer."

Jack turned to look at the sun. He caught sight of the tree house sitting on top of a snowdrift, not far away.

Jack tied a knot in the wind-string. He tied three more, and the sleigh came to a stop at the foot of the snowdrift.

Merlin looked at them. "On the winter solstice, you

showed great courage," he said. "You endured storms and terror and extraordinary cold. You reunited the Ice Wizard and the swan maiden. And perhaps most important, you retrieved my Staff of Strength. I thank you."

"Sure," Jack and Annie said modestly.

"You have done much for the kingdom of Camelot on your last four missions," said Merlin. "On your next adventure, you will have a mission back in your world—in real time, not in the time of myth and magicians."

"We will call for you again soon," said Morgan.

"Great!" said Annie.

Jack and Annie climbed out of the sleigh. They looked back at Teddy and Kathleen. "I hope you will help us with our next journey, too," said Annie.

Teddy smiled. "If we all work together, we can do anything, aye?" he said.

"Aye!" said Jack and Annie together. Then they turned

and trudged up the snowdrift. At the top, they climbed into the window of the tree house. Once they were inside, they looked back.

The sleigh was gone.

"Bye," Annie said softly.

Jack picked up the small gray stone from the floor. He pointed at the words *Frog Creek* in the wizard's message. "I wish we could go there," he said.

The wind started to blow.

It blew harder and harder.

Then everything was still.

Absolutely still.

*   *   *

Jack opened his eyes. They were back in the Frog Creek woods. No time at all had passed while they'd been gone. It was almost twilight. Snowflakes fell like tiny feathers outside the tree house window.

Annie shivered. "I'm cold," she said.

"Here—take my scarf," said Jack. He pulled off his scarf.

"No, you need it," said Annie.

"No, take it. I'll be okay." Jack put his scarf around Annie's neck. "What will you tell Mom when she asks about *your* scarf?" he asked.

"I'll just tell her the Sisters of Fate took it as payment for telling us how to find the eye of the Ice Wizard in a hole in the Hollow Hill," said Annie.

"Right," said Jack, laughing.

"We'd better get home before dark," said Annie. She started down the rope ladder. Jack followed her.

As they stepped onto the ground, Jack remembered the wind-string. "We forgot to give this back," he said. He reached into his pocket and pulled out the string. "I guess Merlin's magic took the sleigh back to Camelot."

Jack and Annie looked at the string for a moment. "Untie a knot," Annie whispered.

Jack took off his gloves and untied a knot. He held his breath and waited. Nothing happened. He gave Annie a little smile. "I guess in our world, it's just a piece of string," he said.

Jack put the string back in his pocket. He and Annie started walking over the snowy ground between the trees. As they walked, Jack looked for Teddy's and Kathleen's footprints. But they were completely gone.

Jack and Annie moved out of the woods and down their

street. They saw Christmas tree lights sparkling in people's houses and candles shining in windows.

Their boots squeaked as they crossed their snow-covered yard. When they got to the stairs of the porch, Jack stopped. He stared in astonishment.

Annie's red woolen scarf was draped over the railing of the porch.

"I don't believe it!" said Jack.

"I do!" said Annie.

They hurried up the stairs and Annie grabbed her scarf. "Look!" she said.

She held up the scarf to show Jack. There was a tiny picture woven into it: a picture of him and Annie and two white wolves.

Jack was speechless.

"Cool, huh?" said Annie. She gave Jack back his scarf. Then she tied her scarf around her neck. She tucked the part

with the picture under her jacket collar.

The front door opened. A delicious smell wafted out from the house.

"Hi!" said their mom. "The cookies are ready. Come inside and get warm!"

图书在版编目（ＣＩＰ）数据

寒冰巫师：英、汉/(美)奥斯本著；蓝葆春，蓝纯译.—武汉：湖北少年儿童出版社，2010.3

(神奇树屋：典藏版)

书名原文：Winter of the Ice Wizard

ISBN 978-7-5353-5015-2

Ⅰ.寒… Ⅱ.①奥…②蓝…③蓝… Ⅲ.儿童文学—短篇小说—美国—现代—英、汉 Ⅳ.Ⅰ712.84

中国版本图书馆 CIP 数据核字(2010)第 040525 号

This translation published by arrangement with Random House Children's Books, a division of Random House, Inc.

Book #32-**Winter of the Ice Wizard** Text copyright ⓒ 1992 by Mary Pope Osborne

Magic Tree House™ is a trademark of Mary Pope Osborne, used under license.

著作权合同登记号：图字：17-2006-050

神奇树屋典藏版 32——寒冰巫师

原　　著：[美]玛丽·波·奥斯本
责任编辑：叶 珺　何 龙
整体设计：一壹图文

出 品 人：李 兵
出版发行：湖北少年儿童出版社
经　　销：新华书店湖北发行所
印　　刷：湖北恒泰印务有限公司

规　　格：880×1230　1/32　6.75 印张
印　　次：2010 年 4 月第 1 版　**2016 年 8 月第 10 次印刷**
书　　号：ISBN 978-7-5353-5015-2
定　　价：16.00 元

业务电话：(027)87679179　87679199
http://www.hbcp.com.cn